THEY DON'T SEE A THING.

THE COMPACT

JUSTINA LUTHER

The Compact

I dedicate this book to God who gave me the words and to my dear friend Yolanda Allard, an excellent author and invaluable friend, who without her, this book would make no sense.

The Compact

Chapter One

5:30 a.m. September 1, Springfield, Connecticut

People say I'm a girl you can't trust. They say I invent stuff. Maybe they're right, or maybe I'm the one who sees the world clearly.~ Angela Miller

Do most sixteen-year-olds wake each morning to question what happened while they slept, or is it just a me deal? Snuggled beneath the ebony quilt my grandmother made me before my birth, I don't want to pull myself out of my warm nest, but I do and untangle my legs from the sheets. Black is a weird color to choose for a baby gift, but maybe she guessed it would be one of my

The Compact

favorites. When I take a deep breath, I smell the bacon Dad fries in the kitchen.

I slip into the bathroom across the hall and run a comb through my short, wavy. chestnut hair while the hem of my white nightgown swishes at my ankles. Dark circles rim my chocolate eyes. *Why?* A yawn cracks my jaw. *Isn't eight hours enough?*

"Angela!" Dad calls from the foot of the stairs. "Are you leaving your bed today or what? You'll be late for school!"

In my room, the sun bounces off the deep purple walls of my bedroom, and I yank open my antique wooden dresser, pull out the day's clothes, and tug my nightgown over my head before I shimmy into a pair of ripped jeans and a plum colored hoodie. *Purple's Mom's favorite color. I guess she's where I come by the love of it. Maybe she'll*

The Compact

visit today or Sophie. Baby sisters are the best. I miss them.

The wooden staircase creaks underfoot with each step, and I wonder how I ever manage to sneak out of the house at night without waking the neighborhood. *Will tonight be the night The Shadow kills someone?*

"Earth to Angela."

My head snaps up when I shuffle into the kitchen, and I find Dad waving a metal spatula, a dishtowel slung onto one shoulder.

"You'll bust my experiment if you keep on autopilot."

"Huh?" My attention focuses on the set of glass tubes on the wooden stand a few inches from my hip. "Sorry," I mumble, moving away to head for the table.

The Compact

"No harm done if it makes it to school with me." His hazel eyes shine. There isn't anything that makes him light up quite like his students.

"What made you want to be a teacher?" I rip off a piece of one of the bagels he laid out to pop it into my mouth.

A crease forms between his brows while he flips the bacon out of the pan and onto a paper towel lined plate. "You did. Plus, I needed a change of scenery once the rock quarry closed."

"Why?"

He chuckles and sets the food on the table before going to grab the orange juice from the fridge. "You're full of questions today. Eat or we'll both be late!"

I know better than to keep probing and pull my journal out of my backpack to

The Compact

scribble a few notes. "I hope Ronni is at school today."

Dad flinches but doesn't say anything.

***

6:45 a.m. September 1, Springfield, Connecticut

The sun streaks the sky with stripes of orange, yellow, and hot pink while I walk to school, the morning's breeze cool on my cheeks. I wave and nod to my neighbor who's out in her yard playing with her three-year-old daughter. The girl waves, but her mom's eyes widen as if I'd flipped them off. She takes her daughter's wrist and tugs her inside.

The Compact

Someday, they'll have a parade for me. I dig into my pocket and pull out the letter Ronni left for me last night.

What up? No movement with The Shadow when I patrolled. Mark my words though, it's planning something for this sad, sleepy town. I can't read its mind, but we can both sense it. Destruction is deliverance; I hope you'll agree with me one day. There's no other way to deal with this, but we'll play it your way for now.

Ronni

My heart skips, and I swear I can hear The Shadow's growl. I roll the sleeve of my sweatshirt to my elbow and run my thumb over the marks my last encounter with it left. The deep gashes early sent me to the hospital, but it killed sheep at the nearby farm. Ronni said we had to check it out.

The Compact

First animals, and then what? Where does it go when the slaughter of an animal isn't enough to calm its anger? A pit opens in my gut, but I smother it. *This town may hate me, but we have to help it. If we can figure out where The Shadow came from, its motivation, we'll be able to get rid of it.*

The breeze whistles through the changing maple trees to send a shiver down my spine. *Fall is early this year. How often has Ronni joked about leveling this place in the middle of the night?* My school comes into view in the distance, it's mortar chipping between the bricks.

***

8:00 a.m. September 1, Springfield, Connecticut

The Compact

Destruction is deliverance.~ Ronni Russo

Ronni... I slump on my desk and doodle my name in the notebook, a note I'll leave for Angela later. At the front of the room, Mr. Beezly bangs his knuckles against the blackboard, but I keep scratching at the paper until a ruler whacks the desk an inch from my nose. "Dude! What's your problem?" I swallow and sit up. *Dang it! I gotta stop doing this.* "Sorry," I clear my throat, "sir."

His lips form a thin line, dark green eyes hardening, his black toupee off center. "What is the answer?" He points to the board.

Come on, dude. You've got this. You have to. I straighten my back and shift in the seat. If I could, I'd glare a hole through the problem, or through *him*, and my issues

The Compact

would be solved. *Negative X.* "Negative X…squared?" *Yes!*

He grumbles and returns to the front of the room.

The pencil in my grasp snaps and one-piece clatters to the floor. A few students peek my way, but most know better and avoid eye contact. I leave it where it lays and pull another from my sleeve. *Fifty more minutes and I'm free.*

***

4:30 p.m. September 1, Springfield, Connecticut

This town can't move beyond its past if it doesn't even understand it.~ Angela Miller

The Compact

I blink, the sun warm on my cheeks while I lean against a fence post, a note clutched in my hand with Ronni's name scrawled on the front. I bite my lip and unfold the paper. "As usual, Mr. Beezly yapped until his jaw unhinged. A gruesome sight, but I made it through. Aced the math problems too." I roll my eyes at the wink Ronni drew beside the line. "I'll ask again, are you sure you want to go through with this *search* of yours? Deliverance is destruction, it's fast and easy too. If we get rid of its source of power, even the whole town, we solve the problem." *Yes, I'm sure. I have to get to the bottom of this. This town can't move beyond its past if it doesn't even understand it, and most are innocent.* I push my bangs off my forehead while a cool breeze stirs my skirt and tilt my head at the tan cowboy boots peeking from beneath the

The Compact

multicolored hem. *What did I do? Change with my eyes shut?* I pinch the bridge of my nose and push off the sun-bleached wood to shuffle down the sidewalk, my day a blur. *Whatever, at least I'm dressed this time.*

My feet drag me toward our old house on Dumont Circle. *Don't go there.* I wag my head to clear the idea. "I have to do this. We have to..." A woman reading a magazine on her front lawn catches sight of me, and I bite my lip and wave. *Yes, talk to yourself. It's not like they don't already think you're insane. What if people are right about us?*

The sun heads for the horizon while gooseflesh covers my arms and the cement beneath my feet rises and falls. I hug my waist, a cold sweat breaking over me while a breeze whistles through the trees. When my phone buzzes in my pocket, my muscles

The Compact

freeze, and I almost fall like one of those fainting goats Sophie loves. Fishing it out, I find a text from Dad.

Dad: Where are you, Angie?

Me: Out for a walk.

Dad: You said you were going to do your homework.

Me: I couldn't get my head into it, so I went for some air. I'll see you soon.

I shove the phone into my pocket again while it buzzes once more and keep moving. The town shifts from upkept to dilapidated with a speed that might shock anyone who hadn't lived here their whole life. Chunks of asphalt are popped out from last Winter and left to litter the street. Give or take a few blurry years, I'd watched this area fall to pieces. Deep patches of dead leaves gather beneath snarled trees, some half dead, others fallen from their lofty

The Compact

places. *Lofty place, are we Shakespeare now?* I giggle and jiggle the thought from my head. Pulling out Ronni's note, I scan it once more. *Why doesn't he want me to do this?* When my stomach flips, I bite my lip. *Deliverance may be destruction, but knowledge is power. If I'm going to save this town, I have to find The Shadow's home. I have to learn where it began.*

I round the corner onto our old street, the concrete sidewalk beneath me completely crumbled out. The once crisp picket fences fallen like a trail of dominoes from one yard to the next. Hazy memories gnaw at me, none of them in focus. They feel like someone else's. I pick my way over uneven ground past the houses to the end of the road, where a squat wrought iron gate blocks off a long dirt driveway. *You'd think*

The Compact

the best house in town could have afforded pavement.

Something growls and breaks the silence. My heartrate spikes. When I whirl and scan the shadowy tree line, I find nothing. My back plastered to the fence; I bite my lip. *Only Ronni can see The Shadow. It could be right here, and you wouldn't know it.* A chill runs up my spine, and I pull out my stun gun. I hop the fence with an eye toward the sky. *Get in, see what shakes loose, and leave.* I gulp, ball my fists, and march down the extended driveway.

The house itself is tucked to the right side of the drive; the property could have held two other houses. *Why did Mom want this much space?*

A twig snaps beyond the tree line which rims the property, and I flinch, peering into the bushes still thick with a mix

The Compact

of maroon and dark green leaves. *Don't linger!* I run to the front door. It's not even locked after all these years, and I stumble over rotted wood into the semi darkness. *I don't know if it's me, or the house, but one of us is definitely cold. Nerves?—No!* I straighten my back and scan the hall. *Where did this lead?* I blink.

"Angela, what are you doing here?" Mom shakes her head and picks her way past rotten floorboards to the kitchen at the end of the hall, an offshoot to the left of it leads to the main living room, a staircase to the second floor at its center. "This place isn't safe. I'm glad I came when I did. This is not a place for my baby girl." She bites her lip and mutters, "Why did she come here? It's not as if our happiest memories live within these walls." She peers at the rear door and wags her head. "No. We don't

The Compact

need to be here." She steps toward the door and hesitates, the lid of a rusted metal trash can visible above the bottom edge of the window. "Let's go out the front." She spins on her heel and rushes for the front entrance once more. "We're getting you home and *not* coming back."

The journey is silent, and people ignore us when we pass. "They've never much liked our family. Said our money was nothing but blood money, but they're wrong. My grandfather earned it fair and square. I can't believe they take this out on you, of all people," she says at the front door of Dad's house.

"Angela? Hon—" His face falls, and Mom beams at him. "Candice?"

She winks. "Happy to see your memory is intact. Wanted to pop in and

The Compact

make sure you're taking care of our girl. I found her at the old house."

He runs a palm down his throat. "It's not safe—"

"I know! I've told her several times. Ronni has too, but she won't listen."

He huffs. "*I've* told you; you can't go there—Angela, are you listening to me?"

I blink. "What?" My brain feels like it's sloshing from one side of my head to the other.

"Dad?"

He studies his shoes, his fists in his pockets. "You have to stay away from the Dumont house, okay?"

"I—" Ice flows through my veins and I bob my head. "Yes, sir."

He must catch the look on my face because he sets a palm on my arm with a soft smile.

The Compact

"Candice brought you home. Why don't you go upstairs and finish your homework? I'll have dinner ready when you're done."

I peek over my shoulder when I head for the staircase while Dad latches the front door. *Thanks, Mom.*

On my bed, I open my journal and jot out a few notes.

Visited the house on Dumont Circle. Mom came and brought me home. Made it inside this time, though. What is it about the house everything wants to keep me away from? Connection to Shadow?

My thoughts go fuzzy, and I tuck Ronni's letter between the pages and push off my bed to take a seat at the compact wooden desk shoved into one corner of my room. I run my fingers on the three sets of

The Compact

initials carved into the seal. "CO, AM, SM. Mom, me, and Sophie." Yawning, I pull out my workbook and tuck into the ten-page packet of math homework Mr. Beezly sent home.

The Compact

Chapter Two

3:00 a.m. September 2, Springfield, Connecticut

Angela will get herself killed if she doesn't stop poking into The Shadow's business.~ Ronni Russo

The moon still casts the world in a soft glow when I throw off the covers and pry open the bedroom window. I hold my breath, watch the door, and strain my ears to see if he'll come. *The last thing I need is to be caught on my way out.*

When the hall light doesn't appear beneath the door, I hop out the window onto the course shingles of the roof and crouch for a moment before I shut it. *Angela will get herself killed if she doesn't stop poking*

The Compact

into The Shadow's business. I raise the hood of my sweatshirt with a grunt and scoot to the edge of the roofline, climbing onto the nearby tree and descending the strong branches to the ground. "Nothing will stop her," I grumble. *Nope.* "I wish she wasn't dead set on saving this crappy town. They're in on it, but she doesn't want to accept it. What happened couldn't—" I dig my nails into my palms. "You have a job to do. Do it, keep her safe, and get home."

I slip through the night, my head on a constant swivel in case *he* appears. *In the middle of a neighborhood with kids around is not ideal.* When I reach the tree line at the edge of town, I throw off my hood and run. The night air slips through my hair.

When the forest breaks again, the abandoned cement factory comes into view and my gut lurches. *I should have brought*

The Compact

this place to the ground when I had a chance. "Let's get this done with."

As silently as I can, I cover the hundred feet through weed eaten cement to the one broken glass window. I pull my sleeves onto my palms to protect them and boost myself into the building. Glass crunches beneath my feet and the sound echoes off the abandoned walls. The shadows stir, and my gut lurches as the dank air fills my senses. *He's here.*

A laugh bounces off the walls, and I let out a slow breath to calm my pounding heartbeat. *Find the doll, and you're out of here.* I stick to the chipped cinderblock walls, rough beneath my fingers. With it at my back, it's one less angle to worry about him coming from. *Where was it?* The moldy smell of neglect makes me dizzy. *The walls would scream if they could. How can one*

The Compact

building hold this many evil memories and stay quiet?

A rat scampers in front of me, his claws scratching the cement. I jump away and send my foot into a puddle of ice-cold rainwater from a gaping hole in the roof above my head. I chomp my lip to keep from screaming, surprised when I don't taste blood. *Hurry.* My instincts lead me through wide corridors past massive hunks of equipment outlined in the low light and left to rust. At last, I spy the office door at the top of a rusted flight of stairs; a few of the steps hang from one corner. *That's where she is.* My gut flips at the wide expanse of open space between me and where I have to get for the stupid toy. *If she wasn't dead set on saving this—* From the shadows, a deep breath sends my heart into my throat, the stank of rotted garbage giving me a gut

The Compact

punch. I pull the collar of my sweatshirt onto my nose and manage not to hurl as I crouch at the base of a giant metal drum.

Wait for the hum. I pull myself into a stance like a runner at the starting block. His footsteps echo to come from all sides and make my fight or flight instinct pound at the back of my skull. *Hold it together. Don't let him flush you out.*

The Shadow groans from the other side of the room, and a bench along the far wall creaks beneath his weight. I peek around the drum to find his ten-foot three-inch height illuminated by a shard of moonlight. The festering wounds that dot his bluish-gray body teem with maggots. Short black hair pokes out at odd angles on his head, his white eyes wide while he studies the crack in the ceiling. Thin trails of blood which forever stream from his eyes flow

The Compact

past the gaping hole where a nose once was to collect and drip from his chin while his spider leg like fingers scratch at his jawline. After a moment, he tilts his head backward, resting it against the wall. His low hum vibrates the night with a disconnected tune.

I keep my movements light and my head low as I sprint for the stairs with one eye on him. Not that it's much help when a creature of his nature can shadow warp and end up near anywhere, I don't want him to. At the stairs, I take them two at a time, dodging the ones that have either crumbled away or look like they're about to. His pulse thrums in the air, slow and steady. *Don't get caught. Get the doll and get out.* I hit the metal landing, the whole structure vibrating, and sprint for the door of the office when he stops. Shutting it, I crouch beneath the window, my ear to the pressed wood. *Did he see me?* Silence.

A breeze stirs. and I shudder. The putrid scent of garbage grows stronger while humid air seeps past the edges of the door. I cover my mouth to keep from gagging, and a low chuckle rumbles against the wood.

"Good," he growls. "Good," he says it again and again, his voice muffled until it falls away.

Once the scent fades, I dare a peek through the window to find nothing but the building beyond. I slide down the door to the floor, my cheek against the cool surface until my heartbeat slows. *Keep moving. You have a job to do.* I reach and lower the blinds in case he's still nearby.

Crouched, I tiptoe across the tattered rug crusted with dirt and pull a flashlight from my pocket. *Why do nasty things always*

The Compact

have to live in dusty places? I bite my tongue against a building sneeze.

The beam of my light sweeps the rug and digs into the darkened places. *Where are you, you hunk of junk?* The light swings into a corner beneath the remnants of a plywood desk and a speck of faded brown paint catches my attention. I dig through a thick layer of filth and unearth my prize. The discarded doll gapes at me with the one eye she has left, her mouth frozen open in a silent scream, one arm ripped off her cloth body. I stash her in my backpack, sling it onto my back, and head for the broken window. Rather than go through the monster's lair once more, I jump out of it onto the fire escape and risk another rickety flight of stairs.

I push my legs harder than I ever have, through empty fields and past the

The Compact

sleepy shops at the center of town. The few people I encounter look the other way. By the time I make it *home*, I'm out of breath and soaked in sweat, but my heart soars when I climb through the window and stash the doll beneath the bed, slinging my backpack onto the desk chair. I peel out of my sweaty clothes and shove them into the hamper to tug my sleep stuff on again and hop into bed. *Wait!* I roll my eyes and grab a journal to jot a few quick notes.

***

7:00 a.m. September 3, Springfield, Connecticut

People like him don't deserve The Shadow's wrath, and they're what make this town worth saving.~ Angela Miller

The Compact

"Angela? Honey, are you awake yet? You'll be late for school."

I roll onto my stomach and pull my pillow over my head. *It's too early to be up.*

It doesn't take much time for the hinges on my bedroom door to squeak and my bed to wobble.

"Angela, I know you hear me," Dad says. "Out of bed in the next five minutes, or I'll rip out the blankets and dump a cup of ice on your feet." He pries up the corner of my pillow to beam at me while I scowl which makes him laugh.

When he shuts the door, I grumble and sit up. My body aches. *Am I coming down with something?* I stumble into the bathroom and pull a brush through my hair while a yawn cracks my jaw. When I stretch,

The Compact

my back pops from the bottom to the top. "Am I sixteen or sixty?"

I drag myself into a pair of jeans and a graphic T-shirt which makes Dad wag his head when I make it to the kitchen.

"You'll freeze!"

"I'll manage."

He tosses a packet of strawberry toaster pastries my way, and I catch them midair. "Nice." He beams. "Grab your stuff. I'm driving you to school today."

"You are?"

"Yep, you slept in, which breaks the rules, your walking privileges are revoked for the day. I'll drive you home this afternoon too—"

I gulp and shift my weight from one foot to the other. "I can walk myself home. If I don't, I have to be there for an extra half hour."

The Compact

He throws an arm around my shoulders to usher me toward the door and plants a kiss on the top of my head. "I don't make the rules, kiddo—"

"In fact, you do."

His eyes go wide. "Terrifying." With a wink, he slips my backpack off of a kitchen chair and nudges me outside.

"I—I don't remember bringing—"

"It's okay, honey. I grabbed it on the way out of your room."

I gulp and tuck my hair behind my ear. "Thanks." Once I'm settled into the passenger seat of Dad's maroon truck, I rest my head against the window while the town buzzes by us.

Within ten minutes, we're pulling into the school's gate which Bill, the ancient security guard, is halfway through pulling shut.

The Compact

"I told you so," Dad says.

When Bill spots us, he beams and pulls the gate open. "Cutting it close, aren't we?"

"Someone couldn't be bothered to leave her dreams." Dad jerks his head toward me.

When the man chuckles, I lift one corner of my mouth. *I always liked Bill. Seems to be a good dude...people like him don't deserve The Shadow's wrath, and they're what make this town worth saving.*

My thoughts must plaster themselves on my face because his smile fades. "Everything okay, kiddo? Why so glum?"

A car horn sounds behind us, and Dad checks the rearview. "Is that Bethany?"

"Ms. Pewtonson? Yeah, she's covering for Mr. Beezly today," Bill says.

The Compact

Pain builds between my brows, and I open the pastries in my lap to nibble them.

"Poor guy has the flu."

Dad waves once more and drives us to the rear where the teachers park. When he hops out, he grabs his briefcase out of the bed. "Meet me here after school. Do you understand me? When I get to the truck, I want to find you here."

I bite my tongue to keep from saying, or?

"If you don't, you're grounded for two weeks."

My heart drops. "I can't be!" *The town may not be here in two weeks if I'm at home!*

He tweaks my nose. "Have a nice day, sweetie."

I tip my chin to the clouds and let out a slow breath. From the corner of my vision,

The Compact

I catch Ms. Pewtonson watching something from where she waits by her car. When I turn, I pray for the ground to swallow me. *She's watching Dad.* My stomach churns. Before I can spin and run, she calls out to me.

"Angela! Hi, sweetheart. Walk to class with me?"

I hug my waist and wish Ronni was here. *Where are you when I need you? What's worse? A stroll with her, or a week grounded for lack of respect?* Biting my lip, I bob my head and hope she'll chalk up my silence to usual weirdo teen behavior. I follow her a half pace behind.

"How are you? I haven't seen you in a while."

As we near the back entrance, the scent of trash meets my nose and a cold sweat breaks over me while my pulse

The Compact

speeds. I cast an eye to the sky where a cloud covers the sun and grab her elbow to hurry her toward the door. "Storm is coming. We better head in."

Once the door clicks shut behind us, we part ways, and I pray the sun comes out to burn the monster into the shadows again. *If I could see it...I wonder if Ronni can teach me.*

I slip upstream through the hoard of students that crowd the halls, the chatter clashing with my thoughts until I'm dizzy.

"Get out of the way, freak," some jock says and rams his elbow into me.

I ball my fist but focus on the dingy scuffed linoleum. When I make it to my locker, I input my combination and then spin the dial when it doesn't work. "Does everyone in this place enjoy messing with my locker? Or am I imagining it?"

The Compact

"Not the whole school, but ninety-nine percent of it if shuffle and traffic patterns are any indication," a muffled voice from the locker beside me says.

Frowning, I peer between the metal slats into a pair of electric blue eyes. "Who are you, who did you tick off, and how? This locker has been empty for months."

"It's at full capacity at the moment...past it, in fact. A historical volume is currently trying to be too friendly with my gluteus maximus."

"What—you mean you're being goosed by a book?"

"Precisely. It's quite uncomfortable."

I fumble with the lock. "What's your combo, kid?"

"Twenty-four, ten, eighteen."

When the lock pops and I pull open the door, a gangly but petite set of arms and

The Compact

legs collapses in a tangled heap on the floor, a patch of carrot shaded curls on top of it all.

"Thank you." The boy says and dusts himself off, standing to offer a handshake.

I bite my lip to keep from laughing, a cherry bowtie at his throat. Thick suspenders hold his pants in place. "Nice to meet you, kid."

"Oliver Wendel, at your service. I'm a freshman. What year are you?"

"Sophomore, Angela." I peer at his round eyes and full cheeks. "How old are you?"

His face falls. "Am I truly so obvious?" When I tilt my head, he crosses his arms. "I am a freshman; however, I skipped two grades…rats. Here I, after hours of consideration, chose to skip two grades instead of the four I'm capable of, believing

The Compact

myself more apt to blend into a freshman class."

Dear sweet Oliver…you will not blend into anything, anywhere…ever. I pat his arm. "Use a few less expensive words if you want to blend and maybe lose the bowtie."

He straightens it. "Ah, my choices in fashion were mentioned previous to my impromptu and detailed tour of my locker…" He reaches to tug at a wedgie.

I chew my bottom lip and bob my head. *This kid will be eaten alive here.* "Listen, spend the least time in the halls you can. Grab your stuff and take the long way to the classes through the East halls. The flooring is janky in there. No one with any social clout will be caught dead there. It's safe."

The Compact

He cranes his neck to peer beyond me, and I roll my eyes. *You can't force someone to take advice.* I shift my attention to my locker and pop off the lock to hook it on my pocket.

"What a clever notion." He watches it dangle.

"I lose stuff. When it's important, I keep it on me."

"Forgetful?"

"Sure."

When the door swings open, a folded piece of paper flutters to the ground. *It must be important if he took the time to stash it here.* I scoop the paper off the linoleum and start to open it before I realize Oliver is still staring at me. I tuck it into my pocket and grab my math book.

"Do you have a boyfriend?"

"What?"

The Compact

"The name Ronni was written on there. It sounds like a male name as opposed to feminine—though I don't mean to be politically incorrect by assuming—"

I snort. "You're fine, kid—Oliver. Ronni is…someone special to me."

His eyes twinkle, and he pops onto his toes. "Ah, shy I gather. Fair enough." He pulls a few books from his locker and cranes his head one way then the other. "The East wing is which direction?"

I raise a brow. "East."

"Of course." His cheeks redden. "I must admit, directional skills are not one of my strong points. Left or right?"

I tip my chin, "Retrace yourself down the hall, take a right, straight on, take two lefts. Keep going until the floor looks like this." I point to what's at our feet.

The Compact

He heads on his way, and I grab my stuff. A part of me wants to rip open Ronni's letter then and there, but I can't risk it. Not yet.

The Compact

Chapter Three

4:30 p.m. September 3, Springfield, Connecticut

I've been trying to tell you something was coming.~ Angela Miller

I hop into Dad's truck and lock the doors. The clouds still blot out the sun while the still air presses in, but I'd rather see the fog of The Shadow's breath than be caught without warning. *You never know where he might be with the whole town cloaked in shadows right now.* A chill darts up my spine, and I scan the world outside. Each shifting blade of tall grass which rims the school's property makes me jolt. I pull out Ronni's note and unfold it.

The Compact

The Shadow is planning something—

You don't say, Captain Obvious.

—I went by the cement factory and he caught me.

My pulse stutters.

He cornered me in a room, but he didn't do anything. He could have ripped me to pieces but let me live. We need to put an end to him. Destruction is deliverance.

I scribble my reply beneath his note and fold the page again to hide in our secret place.

"Homework?"

With a yelp, I crumple the note while Dad swings open the driver's side door.

"Everything okay, kiddo? I haven't seen you jump that hard in a while."

The Compact

I force the corners of my mouth into a happy angle. "All good."

"Is—uh—is Ronni…"

"No—I'm…No. I'm tired. Can we go home now?"

***

10:00 p.m. September 4, Springfield, Connecticut

He'll catch me before I can make it.~
Angela Miller

I'm out of my mind. This much I'm positive of while an early autumn breeze whistles through the trees to shake more leaves to the ground. The moon hangs heavy in the sky, her light shines bright, though darkness still surrounds me. I rub the last of

The Compact

the dreams from my eyes and arch the beam of my flashlight across the abandoned dirt road. *Why did I fall asleep after dinner? I have to get this letter to Ronni. There's no time to waste.*

A twig snaps behind me and I spin, holding out the knife I carry. "Who's there?"

The air shifts while a few crickets chirp in the stillness. *Why did I leave my stun gun out? I knew Dad would take it.* I strain my ears but catch nothing beyond them. In the low light, I see no parting grasses or pebbles kicked across the pavement. Each place the beam of my light hits leaves me convinced The Shadow is a pace beyond. I wag my head. *You're paranoid and tired. Keep moving. The longer you're out here, the higher your odds of a run in.* I spin on my heel to keep going when a snow furred cat saunters out from

The Compact

behind a snarled maple tree. A fat dead rat dangles from its jaws. The cat cocks its head, round golden eyes blink in the moonlight. Its rosy nose bears one black dot.

"Shoo kitty, it's not safe out here at night," I hiss. "Go back to town where you belong. You'll be eaten up by a bear in a minute." It brings its meal to me, rumbling while it rubs against my leg. I nudge it. "Go! Get out of here."

It jumps away and focuses on something in the distance. It drops the rat, its back arched, fangs bared as it hisses and growls. I gulp while the putrid stench of decay fills my senses. For a moment, I'm frozen.

Something scrapes along the dirt road while my heart hammers to send the blood into my legs again, and I bolt. *I'm too far from home! He'll catch me before I can*

The Compact

make it. Where do I go? I pump my legs faster and harder. I push myself for all I'm worth. My lungs ache. I plunge off the road and into the tree line and pray a few obstacles will at least slow it. Low branches claw at me and scrape my cheeks, catching on my clothes and hair while I dive between them. I would scream for help, if I trusted anyone might come, but all I'd draw in is it.

The world groans behind me. If I dared to peek, I'd find the trees parting in the wake of the invisible. Branches the size of my leg snapped off as if they were nothing. When the forest ends, I stumble out of the trees and scurry through a hole in the fence line. The metal rattles while I climb a bank of discarded stone. I slide down the other side while a stray shard slices my palm, and I bite back the yelp that rises in my throat when I sprint for the quarry

The Compact

worker's break house. I swear its breath warms my neck, fingers sliding through my hair while it toys with me, letting me stay out of reach. I pour everything I have into my legs.

A maze of pipework lies between me and shelter. Vaulting the first of the water pipes protruding from the ground, I leap the next, then another. My arms ache by the time I've jumped the last one. I've barely landed when the toe of my shoe catches on a metal rod jutting from the dirt. I crash to the ground; gravel bites my cheek. I yank my foot, but it doesn't budge. *Come on!* Grabbing my pantleg, I tug, and my ankle pops. I scream, white hot fire shooting up my leg while my foot slides free. When I try to stand, it twists at an inhuman angle. My whole leg throbs. Tears cloud my vision, and I collapse once more.

The Compact

I curl into a ball, eyes shut tight, and cover my head with both arms. The ground beneath me shakes while the air warms with the same rank scent. *No. No, no, no.*

The world stills until a spider leg presses against the base of my skull. The Shadow's hairy fingers brush my arms, legs, sides, and through my hair. The creature studies each inch of me I can't pull into my protective ball. I dare not move and hold my breath for fear it may change its mind, and I become dinner, the memory of its fang in my arm sharp in my mind. I blink and all at once, the closeness of the air vanishes, the scent of death gone with it.

I risk a peek from beneath my arm and find the empty night, the moon at its zenith. *Did I pass out?* The pipes are a few yards away, skid marks in the dirt lead from them to me. *It dragged me?* My gut rolls.

The Compact

The windows of the outbuilding are shattered and the note from Ronni lays a few feet away, words scrawled in red. I rise onto my knees and warmth trickles down the inside of one thigh. The sharp scent of ammonia hits my nose while I cry. Shaking, I crawl to the paper. "Is that…blood?" I shudder and check the cut in my palm to find my blood smeared down my wrist.

September 18. Learn the truth.

I blink at the note and my mind swims. *Two weeks. What does it mean?* Exhaustion pulls at me, my arms and legs shaking while my ankle throbs. I rub my forehead and crawl toward shelter. *When the sun rises, I'll try to sound the cave-in alarm. See if it even still works.* Inside, I lock the door and curl beneath one of the old desks, massaging my aching ankle.

The Compact

***

7:00 a.m. September 5, Springfield, Connecticut

Deliverance is destruction.~ Ronni Russo

My jaw drops when I take in the scene in the morning light. I'd planned to check our usual drop spot at the quarry, but the sight I found left my blood to boil. The busted-out window and blood on Angela's palm is enough to tell me who's to blame. I grit my teeth and stagger to my feet; her bad ankle makes the situation near impossible. *What was she thinking?* I glare and clench my fists. "Don't go out at night. There are rules for a reason," I mutter beneath my breath. "You can't *see* it." I run a palm down my face and read her reply at the

The Compact

bottom of my note. "Figure out what he wants? Why he's here? Where he comes from? What's his plan?" My voice rises with each word. *Are you out of your mind?* "Here's an idea, instead of opening whatever can of worms this is, we go with my plan and blow the place to pieces." *There are some people here worth saving.* I shake my head and start the trip to her home. "I'm finding a different drop spot. This one isn't safe anymore. It's too near to his hide out." *What was I thinking?*

    I keep silent the rest of the way to her house and glare at anyone who dares to make eye contact. *Wipe this place off the map. Angela was out there all night, attacked, bloodied, and no one even cared. Her idiot father can't even be bothered to keep her safe. I bet she snuck out the*

The Compact

window right under his nose, and he still hasn't noticed she's missing.

By the time I make it to her place, I'm drenched with sweat and her ankle isn't looking any better. I grit my teeth and drag what feels like dead weight onto the porch. I slam my thumb onto the doorbell.

Mr. Miller answers the door while the smile falls off his face like a lead weight.

"Angela!"

I glare at him and he rocks back on his heels. "Ronni."

"Are you going to help me, or what?"

He takes the weight off the ankle and guides us to the kitchen.

"What happened?"

"The Shadow got her."

His jaw tightens. "Can my daughter speak for herself, please?"

The Compact

I smirk in the silence. "I guess she doesn't want to talk to you. You left her out there all night."

"I didn't know she was gone!"

"Old man," I pinch the bridge of my nose, "I don't want her hurt. I don't know the details but as you see, her palm is sliced open, and her ankle is demolished. Fix it, or I'll make your life a nightmare."

His neck reddens. "Listen here, you punk. Angela will speak for herself, and you'll shut it, do you hear me. Angela?"

I roll my eyes.

"Angela!"

I blink.

"Angela!"

"Stop yelling, Dad!"

***

The Compact

6:40 p.m. September 5, Springfield, Connecticut

People are talking about Ronni?~ Angela Miller

Dad leaves the truck to idle while he pops into the drugstore to grab my prescription. *Pain meds on top of how many prescriptions? Awesome.* I study the bulky gray plastic boot on my right foot. *Who knew a dislocated ankle came with such snazzy gear?* I groan and lean my head against the rear window.

"Angela?"

I jump when someone raps on the glass.

Oliver grins and waves at me, orange curls even more vivid in the evening light.

The Compact

I fight a laugh and unroll the window. "Hello, my neon friend."

He cocks his head for a moment before he chuckles. "I suppose my hair is rather vivid in the particular wavelengths of this light."

"What brings you to town?"

He raises the stack of books he carries. "I learned the town library carried a few tomes of a historical nature the one at our school lacked, thus I made the pilgrimage to its shelves to take them home for the weekend. I missed you at school today and so found it fortuitous when I saw you here."

I point to my boot and then to the crutches flung into the bed of the truck.

His eyes go wide. "How did you injure yourself?"

The Compact

I gulp while my gut twists. "It doesn't matter." Across the street, a group of jocks peer our way. "Listen kid, I like you so here's another social tip—one of the only ones I'm able to give—stay away from me if you want to fit in at school."

"Why?"

"I'm the town nut job."

"You and your boyfriend."

"Excuse me?"

"The Ronni fellow who left you a note in your locker. I overheard the name whispered about the halls, though I wasn't fortunate enough to make his acquaintance."

I swallow the sand in my mouth. *People are talking about Ronni?* "Yeah, him." I comb my fingers through my hair.

"I'm fond of the quirky sort. I enjoy their company."

The Compact

"Listen, if you want to be shoved in your locker less, use smaller words, change your look, and stay far away from me, got it?" I open my door to force him back as Dad comes out of the drugstore with my prescription.

Oliver scurries off when he climbs in. "Didn't want to introduce your old man to your friend?"

He wiggles a brow and I grimace. "Ew! The kid is twelve. He's a transfer. Needed to find the quickest place to get a candy bar, and I told him where the corner store is. On the corner of the block where literally anyone can find it."

His shoulders slump while he starts the car again. "I'm glad you're meeting new people regardless."

The Compact

A heavy silence falls between us, and I shift in my seat. *I sense a storm on the horizon.*

"I didn't appreciate Ronni bringing you home today, *or* the fact you snuck out to begin with."

"You think I control who shows up when I need help?"

His knuckles whiten on the wheel, the vinyl creaking in his grasp. "And why did you need help in the first place? You should have been in bed, at home, asleep."

I fold my arms. "You wouldn't understand."

"Try me."

"The Shadow—"

He groans and slams his palm against the wheel. "This again?"

"It's real, Dad! Ronni has seen it—"

The Compact

"Have you? With your own two waking eyes. Have you seen this *shadow*?"

"*The Shadow*. And not seen, but Ronni—"

"Ronni, Ronni, Ronni. Enough of that name!"

"I care about him, Dad. He's a part of me!"

"Yeah. *A part of you*. No, he is not a part of you."

My vision blurs, and I glare at him. "The Shadow's goal is to destroy this town. It's—it's evil and I—"

"It isn't real, Angela! None of this is—"

"But it is!" I stomp my uninjured foot. "Ronni can see it. He's told me about it, and I've heard it too. I was trying to run away from it!" I raise my bandaged palm while I point to my foot with the other. "Did

The Compact

I do this to myself?" The pain in his eyes douses some of my anger, and I clamp my mouth shut.

He reaches to smooth my hair with one hand. "No, baby. You didn't."

Once home, he grabs my crutches, and I hobble up the front steps onto the porch and flop onto the wooden swing.

He waits by the truck for a few seconds, and I can almost sense him counting to ten.

It's his own fault he doesn't trust his kid. The rest of the town can think what they want, but he knows me. I wipe at my tears.

With the paper bag clutched in one hand, he shuffles toward me, his chin tucked to his collar. "I'll go in and grab you something to wash this down with." He clears his throat. "It's about time for your first dose."

The Compact

The screen door shuts behind him, and I let out a slow breath. *I have to make him understand. I can't see the whole picture on my own, and Ronni is bound and determined this place be destroyed. There has to be another way, but I need help.*

I tilt my head and blink at the ceiling.

"Honey, I…" Mom looks at the boot. "Well, your father is doing a fine job, isn't he?"

He comes outside and groans.

"What a fine how do you do. I leave her with you for what, a day, and she ends up with a broken foot?"

He takes a slow, measured breath and shuts his eyes for a moment before he releases it.

"Candice, how nice of you to drop in."

The Compact

"Drop in, my foot! I ought to be here day and night. I would be if it weren't for you. How do you let our daughter live in this state?"

"*Angela* is fine. *Angela* is in one piece. *Angela* can speak for herself."

Mom waves her arms to the surroundings. "Clearly not! I'm sure, per usual, you've demanded your way on things and won't listen to what she has to say."

"Angela! Candice—dang it! Listen to me and listen good." He points at Mom. "Angela is safe here. She's safe in my care, and she doesn't need you, or Ronni, or anyone else! Just me, and Angela. We're what we need!"

"She *needs* a mother—"

"She doesn't have one!" His eyes water and he scrubs at them with the butt of his palm.

The Compact

"Daddy, what's wrong?"

He shifts, his lip trembling. "Sophie?"

Sophie grins. "Daddy!" She sticks two fingers in the corners of her mouth and pulls when she sticks out her tongue. "Daddy laugh!" she squeals.

Tears roll down his cheeks while he reaches and pats her hair.

"Daddy happy, now?"

He bobs his head. "Daddy is happy now."

"I'm going to go home. Okay?"

"I, no. Wait." He touches her arm before setting on the wooden swing to pull her into a hug.

"Too tight!" she giggles.

He loosens his grip. "I—" He squeezes his eyes shut. "It's been a bit since

The Compact

I've seen you. Stay a minute, and then you can go home with Mommy."

"Okay, Daddy."

He strokes her cheek while silent tears roll. "My strong, brave beautiful girl, you are so missed."

"I'm right here," she giggles.

Pulling away, he kisses her forehead and clears his throat. "Run along with Mommy now, okay? I have to take care of Angela."

"Bye Daddy!" She pulls another face.

The Compact

Chapter Four

8:00 a.m. September 6, Springfield, Connecticut

What did he go through?~ Angela Miller

I blink at the ceiling, my foot in a strange limbo between pain and itchiness. *Is it asleep? Are my nerves dying to leave my leg a shriveled husk that will need removal?* I take a slow, stilted breath. *Drama queen.* I snort. "Possible." My encounter with the shadow plays in my mind once more. "It didn't hurt Ronni, or me. It could have eaten us in a moment, but it didn't. It's not stupid or the whole town would be onto it." *Dad doesn't trust me…but he always has a hard time wrapping his head around what he can't see.* "Ronni is against any attempt to

The Compact

learn about The Shadow, Dad doesn't trust it exists, and then there's September eighteenth. What part does it play? Ronni keeps talking about destroying the town in two weeks, though whether it's hyperbole or a threat…who knows. He wouldn't do it, would he? This town is worth saving. He's talked about burning it to the ground for years." I fold my arms. "It's talk, right? I can't count the notes I've found with those exact words, and yet the town still continues." I rub my forehead and mutter, "It's a miracle the FBI hasn't tracked him down already." *Does he know something I don't?*

A reach above my head and grab my journal off the shelf built into my headboard and rip out one crisp page. I scribble a few cramped notes and question how Ronni can even read my hieroglyphs half the time.

The Compact

If you've learned something I haven't, you have to tell me. What's important about the 18th?

I scratch out the line with a growl. *You can't expect him to tell you. You know how private he is. I swear there's nothing about the guy that isn't hidden behind ten feet of concrete.* I shudder. *What did he go through?* "You need tact." *Or you can find out something on your own, give him the information and force it out of him...* "And we have a plan."

A knock on my door pulls me out of my conversation, and Dad pops his head in. His face lights when he sees me. "Hi, kiddo. How are you today?"

"Tired, cranky, and in pain."

He pouts. "What do you say to a bit of help with all three?"

"What do you have in mind, Pops?"

The Compact

"It's Saturday, what about a reprieve from chores, a massive cup of coffee with chocolate syrup, cinnamon, and whipped cream the way you enjoy it, but I don't let you have, and the house specialty, prescriptions à la carte with a side of pancakes?"

I laugh. "Sounds delicious, but I smell a trap, what gives?"

Stepping into the room, he raises both palms in surrender. "You've caught me."

"What's your nefarious plan?"

"To bribe my adventurous teenage daughter into staying off her foot for forty-eight hours minimum."

I bang a fist on my mattress with a groan. "The doctor didn't say anything about—"

"I know he didn't, but I am."

The Compact

"Come on, Dad! I'll go crazy if I have to stare at the same four walls for two days."

"Hey, you're lucky you're not staring at these walls for a month after the stunt you pulled. Not to mention the destruction at the quarry."

"That was—"

"Yeah, yeah, The Shadow." He pinches the bridge of his nose and puffs out his cheeks. "Enough, we're not having that conversation again. I believe you believe what you say, but to claim some creature, no one but Ronni can see stalks the town for who knows what reason, is too much. You have stretched and pulled my imagination beyond its limits, and I've indulged you out of necessity. Enough is more than enough. Stay put; I'll be back with everything soon."

The Compact

He caves into himself as he leaves, his eyes taking on the distant sadness he often wears.

"Daddy, are you okay?"

Pausing, he turns and sighs. "Yeah, baby. Daddy's okay."

***

1:30 p.m. September 6, Springfield, Connecticut

Maybe if this town loved books more, they'd listen when people try to save their lives.~ Angela Miller

I yawn and open my eyes, my discarded breakfast scraps gone, a plastic wrapped sandwich in their place on my nightstand with a note card beside it.

The Compact

Gone to help Mr. Beezly with some car repairs. Be back by dinner.

Love,

Dad.

I check the clock and throw my legs off the side of my bed, their momentum pulling me up while my head swims. "If Dad can go out, I can too," I say when the room stops spinning. *Wouldn't have to, if he'd let us have a computer in the dang house.*

I toss on my coat, lace my left shoe, and grab the sandwich. Downstairs, I flip on the TV for a quick weather check and sigh in relief when I see clear skies. "If I'm home again in a couple of hours, I shouldn't run into it." My stomach twists. *You can't let The Shadow make you into an agoraphobic. You have enough to deal with.* In the garage, I dig my bike out from behind the garbage

The Compact

cans and study the tiny pedals. It might be comical if it was any other situation. I swing my leg over the seat, half of my booted foot fitting on the teensy plastic square. *I'll have to try to remember to thank Dad for insisting on the closed toed model.* "Here goes nothing."

I kick off and drive my bike forward with my uninjured foot. "Do not lose track of time at the library, Angela," I mutter beneath my breath. "Whatever holds The Shadow in check, you can't trust it to continue…learn the truth." My stomach flips, and I take a deep breath and keep my focus trained straight ahead on my way into town. When I pass a group of kids from school, I pedal faster.

"Freak!" they call after me. "Stay in the basement where you belong, loser!"

The Compact

Deliverance is destruction. I wag my head. "Learn the truth. Dad, Bill, Oliver, and countless other innocent people deserve that much. Heck, *I* deserve it. If Ronni destroys the town, he'll destroy us all." *He's held off because of me...*

My booted foot aches by the time the library comes into view, protesting even more when I have to stand on it while I secure my bike on the rack.

Our town library is one story, half the size of the fire station and twice the size of the one at school. *Maybe if this town loved books more, they'd listen when people try to save their lives.* I shove off the idea, wrap my chain through the wheels, and click the lock into place, the initials CO etched into the metal housing. *Love you, Mom.*

Inside, the air is still, the world outside too cool to turn on the air, and not

The Compact

warm enough for the heater. I pull at the collar of my shirt, but head to the rear toward the two computer bays. The bulky hunks of junk are at least a decade old and sluggish as a snail when I hit the power button on the tower. When at last it comes to life, I pull up the one search engine allowed and stare at the keyboard. "September eighteenth is too vague a search term, too many years have had one…even in this town." I snort. Instead, I search for creatures. I input everything Ronni ever described to me, adding in my own experiences. Pulling a piece of paper from my pocket, I jot a quick note to Ronni and ask him once more to teach me how to see it. *There has to be some way. Even he says he couldn't always—what if it chose to reveal itself to him?* The idea sends a shiver up my spine. "Focus."

The Compact

The screen fills with creepy stories and out of focus images. Each of them fits in its own way, but none of them are it. "The Shadow doesn't abduct kids, that I'm aware of. It hasn't killed anyone, yet—again that I know of…" *What has he done so far? Killed sheep? Ronni said it did.*

"You appear lost in a world of your own creation."

I jolt and blink at a pair of electric blue eyes. "Oliver?"

"Wonderful recall." He beams. "Hello, Angela."

"I told you to stay away from me to blend in."

He plops into the seat beside me. "Yes, but upon further consideration, I question why I ought to reject the friendship of someone who is of value in favor of those who care only for themselves."

The Compact

"You realize you sound like *Spock*, right?"

He snickers and ducks his head. "It's highly possible. *Star Trek* is a favorite of my father's. I've watched it since before I was capable of speech."

And an explanation is found.

"If the truth be told; however, it's history which owns my heart more than the technology and adventures of tomorrow." He peers at my screen. "And it seems stories of a darker and more fantastical nature pique your interest?"

I swallow and minimize the page. "Yeah—I...do you do a lot of research about history?"

He beams and bobs his head. "I especially enjoy researching battles of the past. My current obsession is the Civil War."

The Compact

"If someone wanted to find an event that happened on a specific date, but didn't have certain information, how might they go about it?"

"What keywords do you have?"

"September eighteenth…"

"Of what year?"

I bite my lip and raise a shoulder.

He scratches his chin. "It's far too wide a net to cast. What about specific details of said event? A battle, a general's name, or even a location?"

I rub my throat. *This was an awful idea. The last thing I need to do is scare him.* I force a smile. "Thanks anyway. I'm sure I can find it."

He scowls. "I'm certain you're aware torture is against the Geneva Convention. You can't dangle something like this in front of someone when there is obviously a story

The Compact

to be found and coyly pull it away. It is not my intention to be quarrelsome or impolite; however, it is my earnest desire to assist you." When I open my mouth to argue, his eyes flash.

"Didn't your mother ever teach you it's rude to pry into other people's business?"

"*You're* the one who asked *me*!"

"I've also *asked* you to leave me alone and it seems, what's the word you'd use for it? Hypocritical of you to say I'm rude when you've chosen to ignore me."

His lips form a thin line while he sinks into his seat, his cheeks flushing. He stares at the floor, and I take a slow, deep, breath.

Great job.

"I request to be your friend, Angela. If I may. My family hasn't been in town for

The Compact

much time, and you witnessed the way my first day of school progressed. I apologize for my forward mannerism and—how did you word it? Expensive vocabulary? I don't mean to annoy you; however, my mother has tasked me with making friends here. For those I am loyal to, I do my utmost, and I think I am capable of learning to be—"

I touch his arm. "I get it."

"I also tend to speak a great deal, don't I?"

Laughing, I give him a squeeze. "A bit, but it means I don't have to, which I don't mind."

He grins, and I let my hand drop.

"Listen, I'd be lying if I said I couldn't use some help, but…" I scan the room to make sure no one is listening and lower my voice. "You have to promise not to tell anyone what I'm about to say."

The Compact

His lower lip juts out. "Not even my parents?"

I pinch the bridge of my nose. "If you want them to say you're insane, tell them."

He tilts his head. "My interest is piqued."

It already was, or we wouldn't be having this conversation. "This town…it isn't…normal."

"Mathematically speaking—"

"What? No—what does math have to do with anything?"

He looks at me like I'd asked him if the sky is up and the ground down. "There are formulas for everything. Mathematically speaking, everything has a mathematical norm. Even those which are not deemed normal."

The Compact

I rub my forehead. *This will be impossible.* "Ollie—can I call you Ollie?"

"I'd rather you refrained."

"Oliver, when I say normal, I mean things the scientific community deems normal. What can be seen, felt, and touched by the majority of society."

"Ah, trees, wind, polymer compounds. I follow."

"Yeah. This town faces something that can't be seen by most."

His mouth drops open while his head tilts to one side. "What about touched?"

I shiver pulling away before I catch myself. "You don't want it to touch you."

"It? Wait, for it to make physical contact with someone indicates a sentient being."

I bob my head while my heart hammers against my ribs.

The Compact

His eyes widen, and he bounces in his seat while he grabs the edges and leans forward. "Is it sasquatch? Tell me we're chasing a sasquatch!"

"Shhh!" I scan the room, no one seeming to have noticed his outburst except the librarian. When she catches sight of me with him, she glares at me but stays where she is, putting her nose into her paperwork once more. "Keep your voice down," I hiss. "There's a reason people think I'm insane. I'd rather keep you from the same trap, alright?"

"Okay, it must be another cryptid."

"I have no idea what it is, but it told me—"

"It can talk?"

"Among a bunch of other terrifying details about it, yes."

"What does it look like?"

The Compact

I grab a blank piece of paper and a pencil to do a rough sketch of what Ronni has always described.

His face pales. "What are those?" He points to the creature's fingers.

"They feel like hot dog sized tarantula legs." I shudder. The memory of them searching me sends a wave of panic through me.

His top lip curls in disgust. "Is the rest of the creature covered in hair? What are those spots?"

"No, and somewhere along the line it was injured, or it's diseased. Those wounds haven't healed."

He scratches his head and studies the paper. "A creature with hairy fingers and smooth skin which doesn't easily die—one may assume—but can be damaged with slow or no healing." He nudges the paper

The Compact

away and leans into his seat. He searches me instead.

Well, he hasn't run yet... Here goes nothing. "And it can shadow warp."

He freezes. "Pardon?"

I clear my throat and scratch my arm. "Shadow warp."

"It's—I mean to say..." His mouth opens and shuts though he says nothing more. A part of me expects to see smoke come out of his ears.

I force a smile. "Come on, Oliver, don't tell me I've broken you already."

He wags his head. "It would be foolish for me to say even science comprehends the full mysteries of the universe...I desire to trust you—"

"To be fair, I'm used to the label of crazy. I understand if you don't."

The Compact

He pats my arm before he flushes red and pulls away his hand. "I won't call you crazy, but do you have any proof you might show me?"

The Compact

Chapter Five

2:40 p.m. September 6, Springfield, Connecticut

Sometimes, seeing is believing.~ Angela Miller

I don't know what else to do, or where to take Oliver for the *proof* he's asked for, so we hop on our bikes and pedal. I take him through the center of town, past restaurants, and shops until the paved roads switch to dirt.

"Where are we headed?"

A cold breeze whistles through the trees while their shadows crowd the path. "I'll tell you when we get there," I say and keep my head on a swivel. *If this kid gets hurt, the town will say I did it.* The idea

The Compact

drops the bottom out of my stomach. "If I tell you to run, do it. You got it?"

"Why—"

"Wrong answer. The Shadow shows up, and there's no time to explain. Run, you hear me?"

He rides beside me and glances at the darkness that rushes past our tires. "Shadow? What you showed me had substance and shape why—"

"Ronni my—my boyfriend, is the only one who can see it."

"But you said you've seen it."

I shake my head. "Sight is the one sense I haven't experienced The Shadow with."

A shard of sunlight cuts through the trees to fall across his face, droplets of sweat trickle from his temples. "Are you aware of what it desires?"

The Compact

"Not yet, that's what I hope you'll be able to help me figure out."

The stench of rot slams into us both, and I hit the brakes to scan the tree line.

"D—didn't you say it smelled rotten?" He gulps and pulls the collar of his shirt to shield his nose.

"Shh!" No matter how long I stare, the bushes don't part. The tall grasses rustle, but don't compress. "I don't think this is—" The words die on my tongue when my attention falls on a mound of fly infested fur, a snow colored tail the one thing untouched by blood. I cover my mouth and lower the kickstand to hop off my bike.

"What is it?"

The sweet snow colored cat from the night I faced The Shadow. It would be unrecognizable if it not for the traces of gold visible through the clouding of its eyes, and

The Compact

the two dots which peeks through the dried blood crusted on its nose. Its guts lay scattered on the forest floor.

"Did—did The Shadow kill it?"

Turning my back on it, my vision clouds, and I bob my head. *Sometimes seeing is believing.*

"But how can we be certain?" He has a white knuckled grip on the handlebars of his bike, his skin ashen. "A wild animal might have—"

I shake my head. "Wild animals eat everything with something tiny, and they start with the soft bits. This wasn't done by any animal, and any other animal can smell the evil on it. That's why they don't touch it." He makes a cautious move forward, and I put my bandaged palm on his arm. "Do yourself a favor and don't." I open my

The Compact

mouth and take a deep breath. "Let's keep going."

The rest of the way, we ride in silence while my heart aches. *Why?* When we pull up to the hole in the quarry's fence, we abandon our bikes.

"Has—has it killed before?"

I take his hand and help him over the rubble pile. My pulse spikes from being here again.

"Are you okay?"

When I look at him, his eyes are wide. "What?"

"You zoned out for a second and growled something beneath your breath."

I wag my head and wave him off. "Yeah. I—I want to get in and out. Let's go and then we both need to go home."

The Compact

He trails a few paces behind me. "Has it killed before? You didn't answer my question."

"Some sheep. Ronni has dealt with it more than I have." My mouth waters while my gut rolls.

"Where did The Shadow come from?"

"No one knows."

"You've talked to other people about it?"

I help him over the pipes; to go around them would take us closer to the edge of the pit than I'm willing to risk. I grab his arm when he wavers, his attention glued to my blood in the dirt.

"Is that…"

"Yes." I point to the broken windows. "I think it did that too."

"Think?"

The Compact

"I passed out while it...I don't know, investigated me." I scratch my head.

He shuffles to the drag marks in the dirt for a moment and goes to the windows. "You must have been terrified."

I fold my arms and scuff the toe of my boot in the dirt. "It wrote a note in my blood with the words September eighteenth and learn the truth." I pull the note from my pocket, and he crumples in half, heaving.

The scent of stomach acid and tomato sauce curls the hair in my nose. I move upwind while he wipes his mouth.

"Why would you choose to keep something so grotesque?"

"My memory is crap and sometimes people ask me to prove there's a monster roaming the town."

The Compact

He shoves the note away, and I rock backward a step. "Put it away! Consider me convinced."

It feels like the world stops and my jaw drops. "You *believe* me?"

He scratches his head. "Since the one experiment to definitively prove you're being truthful with me might leave me disemboweled, yes. I do."

Tears sting my eyes. "You don't think I'm crazy?"

His attention shifts from the scuff marks to my bandage, then to the windows, and he wags his head. "Unless you and Ronni are both hallucinating, I don't comprehend how it's possible." He pulls a compact notebook and pencil from the breast pocket of his button-down shirt. "When did the creature first appear?"

The Compact

I peek the way we'd come and take a deep breath of the fresh air. "Ronni first encountered it last year." *No.* "Wait..." I perch on one of the taller pipes. "Ronni talked about a monster when we were kids. Everyone thought it was basic kid stuff...but it might not have been. I'll have to ask him."

"What year was it, the earliest you recall him mentioning anything about monsters?"

The further I dig into the corners of my mind, the more my head aches. I rub my temples.

"I don't know, we may have been, eight? Nine, maybe?"

"Let's say twenty-twelve, give or take a year."

"Yeah."

The Compact

He wags the notepad at me. "No comments to make about the fact my parents don't allow me to have a cellular phone?"

I giggle. "Not a one. I have a dad like that."

He beams. "I knew I liked you." He scratches a few more notes. "I'll dig into local legends, happenings, and cryptid sites. Cross reference the powers you said it had." With a palm, he covers his mouth and takes a moment before he speaks again. "On our way home, I'll examine the carcass a bit closer. The way the creature kills may help to identify it. I'll require you to make a note of anything else you can think of about it too. Any detail might help. Perhaps, if we can identify what crypted species it belongs to and search *it* with the date and local happenings, we might find what it's after."

"And stop it."

The Compact

He gives a sharp bob of his head. "Precisely."

The sun sinks toward the hot pink horizon, and I bite my lip. "We need to get going if we want to make it to safety before dark."

When we reach our bikes, his face lights again. "Hey! What if you, Ronni, and I spend some time as a friend group on Monday?"

A pit opens in my stomach, and I throw a leg onto my bike, not meeting his eye. "Ronni isn't one for hanging out. He likes two things in this world, and other people are not on the list."

"What are they?" He hurries to follow when I kick off.

"Me…and explosives."

***

The Compact

4:00 a.m. September 7, Springfield, Connecticut

To trust people is a dangerous mistake to make.~ Ronni Russo

In the moonlight, I crumple Angela's note after reading it for the fifth time and throw it as hard as I can against the bedroom wall. "More time? What is she thinking?" I growl and pull a piece of paper from my journal and write my reply:

Fine! I'll give you as much time as I can.

I pull a pillow from beneath my head, put it over my face, and scream for all I'm worth. I throw myself out of bed and pace. "Has she lost her mind? Who is this Oliver kid, anyway? Can we trust him? How

The Compact

do we know he won't blab to the whole town and have us put away?" My gut twists, and I hold my temples. "Telling her dad went bad enough! Doesn't she get how much danger this puts us in?"

Opening the door, I tip toe down the stairs past silent rooms to the kitchen and crack open the fridge. I slip my finger against the trigger to stop the light and rummage until I hit a loaf of bread and a package of cheese. Taking them to my room, I stuff my mouth, not tasting either. Flashes of The Shadow dart through my mind. "When did I first see him? Rich. She knows when it happened. She was there. He tried to take off her head. I saved her life and she forgets." I squeeze my fist until the bread pushes through my fingers. "Ungrateful, lousy…the grief I've saved her. You'd think she'd keep her mouth shut and

The Compact

let me do what's gotta be done, but *no*. She has to *understand*. Has to try to get into the mind of some soulless abomination that shouldn't even exist."

I toss the bread in the trash and dig beneath the mattress to pull out my lighter and favorite toy I snuck out of the quarry years ago. I flick the lighter, the flame dancing on and off while I spin the stick of dynamite in my other hand. It's inert now, but on occasion I pull it out and picture whose locker I might leave it in. If Angela wouldn't be the first one they'd go after, I'd have done it years ago when it was still active. *There's no way she'd keep her mouth shut.* I take a deep breath and tip my chin toward the ceiling. *Ride this out. Let Angela run herself ragged chasing leads for something she won't find. She'll come to your side of things eventually. To trust*

The Compact

people is a dangerous mistake to make. There's no doubt about it. I remember the doll beneath the bed. *I'll have to bury it tomorrow, and while I'm at it, I'll make sure this Oliver creep gets a view of The Shadow he won't forget.*

***

10:00 p.m. September 7, Springfield, Connecticut

I shift my weight off my sleeping leg, hidden behind the bushes outside the cement factory. *Any time now, twerp.* I keep my breath quiet, a faint scent of garbage on the wind. The last thing I want to do is bring The Shadow out of the building and onto *my* head.

The Compact

Two minutes past the time the note said, the crunch of gravel draws my attention, the moonlight reflected off the gaudy gold stickers which cover his helmet. *What do you know? The kid came. I'd be impressed if he wasn't trying to stick his nose where it doesn't belong.* I cover my mouth and sink further into the bushes.

When he hops off his bike, he lays it in the dirt, and I roll my eyes. *Yeah, sure Angela. He believes you. Look at the quick getaway he plans on.*

"Angela?" he stage-whispers.

Jerk is quiet as a freight train.

"Angela? Are you here?" he says a bit louder.

The crumbling building groans, something inside clattering and sending Ollie boy a foot off the ground.

The Compact

"Angela?" He reaches into his pocket and pulls out the note I'd left him, reading it beneath a compact flashlight.

The scent of rot grows, and he twists to face the building, taking a few steps toward it.

Something passes by one of the upper windows, and I smirk. *Show time.* The air grows thicker, a cloud passing to blot out the moon. The world plunges into darkness, and I roll my eyes. The thin beam of his light twitches one way then the other.

Heavy footsteps in the dirt echo through the night.

"Angela?" he whispers.

The scent of rot, edged by the tang of blood, presses in, and I can almost hear the creature drool. It growls.

"Angela?"

The Compact

A lighter pair of footsteps shuffles through the dirt, and a clang of metal echoes in what I can only guess is dear old Ollie tripping on his bike while the beam of the light heads for the ground.

"Such a…good child," The Shadow growls.

"Angela? Is that you? This—this isn't humorous."

"Good…Sweet…Child…"

The darkness grows.

***

No matter how I claw at my throat, I can't breathe.~ Angela Miller.

"Oliver?" His voice draws me forward. A moment later, I stumble through the bushes and grope for my bearings.

The Compact

Where am I? The clouds make way for the moon, and the world comes into focus once more. My stomach lurches when I'm engulfed by the scent of decay.

"Angela!"

In the dim light, I can't even tell where it is, or might be, and my heart leaps into my throat.

"Angela, I'm scared."

I grab his wrist and pull him into the tree line. "I'll explain later. Run!"

My stupid boot slows me as I take another path, screaming as I go. *I have to give him a chance.* Branches crack behind me and send a conspiracy of ravens screeching into the night.

"Angela!" Oliver cries.

"Run! Run and don't look back! I'm over here, you abomination! Come and get me."

The Compact

The Shadow warps and lands with a thud at my heels, course, invisible finger spinning and pressing me into a tree. The bark bites into my skull. No matter how I claw at my throat, I can't breathe.

"Good girl… Sweet child," its deep voice laps at my ears. "How pretty…you are. How sweet…you'll taste."

The blood pounds in my ears while my vision blurs.

"Sweet dreams—"

"Get away!"

A beam of light floods my vision, the fingers at my throat vanishing with a hiss.

"Leave her, alone!" Oliver grabs my hand and tugs me away from the trunk. "Come on!"

We run until my lungs ache, stopping in the center of town beneath a streetlight. I collapse against its base, my

The Compact

breath coming hard and fast until I want to throw up.

He braces himself against his knees. "It appears—any—light source—effects the—creature," he pants.

"I guess. Ronni always told me—only the sun did anything to it."

His fists ball at his sides. "Where were you?" He shoves a note beneath my nose.

I blink at the words and shake my head. "Ronni," I growl. Biting my lip, I pinch the bridge of my nose until my thoughts clear. "I didn't send you this, he did."

His eyes widen. "Why?"

"He's protective in the worst way sometimes." I scrub my forehead. "I'll make sure he understands you're on our side. I'm sorry."

The Compact

He tilts his head and peers at me. "You ought to ice your neck. The creature appears to have left several severe welts on you."

"They'll go away soon." I pat his arm and the fear in his eyes drops a notch. Pushing myself to my feet again, I point to his flashlight. "Keep it on and get home. It's not safe for us to stay out here."

"What about you?"

"I'll be fine. I'll see you at school in the morning."

The Compact

Chapter Six

9:00 a.m. September 8, Springfield, Connecticut

He might have gotten him killed...unless that was the idea.~ Angela Miller

I roll onto my side, and my whole-body aches. I almost choke when I see the clock. "I'm late!" I throw myself out of bed and my boot hits the floor with a thud, a fine dust falling from the jeans I'd collapsed into bed in. "Ugh. I'm gross!"

"Knock, knock!" Dad shoulders through the door a moment later. "Surprise—why do you look like a grave digger?"

The Compact

I blink at him and raise a shoulder. "Better question, why are you not panicking that we're late for school?"

One corner of his mouth rises. "It's canceled for the day. Power poles got knocked down on one of the main roads and a crew hasn't gotten to it yet. Rather than have everything function on half the staff, they closed for the day."

"Oh, the joys of small-town life."

"Now, to make a U-turn. Why are you a mess?"

No need to tell him Oliver almost ended up on the front page of the town paper.

"I...uh...couldn't sleep last night. I went to the backyard to...um...watch the moon. It was super bright."

His gaze narrows, but whatever he's thinking, he keeps it to himself. He sets the

The Compact

tray he carries on my lap, a bowl of some generic flakey cereal, an orange, and a glass of milk stare at me. "I thought you could use a bite. Next time, stay inside and open your window to stargaze."

I dig in and hurry bite after bite. "Since school is out, I'll visit my friend Oliver—the new kid in town—and check on him. If that's okay, I mean." I add with a smile.

He pauses while his shoulders inch toward his ears. "Who is he?"

"The kid you saw me talking to the other day. Curly red hair? Outside the drugstore?"

He smiles and his posture relaxes. "Alright, but be home by one, do you understand me?"

"Dad, why—"

"Rather stay home?"

The Compact

"One is wonderful."

He heads for the door before he spins on his heel, one finger in the air. "Oh! You can run an errand for me while you're out too."

I groan. "Always a catch with your kindness." A smile tugs at me.

"It's rule number one in the *Dad of the Year* handbook. The other day, when I helped Mr. Beezly, we were able to do everything except change the spark plugs. I have them and you can drop them off for me."

I rub the back of my neck the orange smooth and cool beneath the palm of my other hand. "Are you sure you can't do that another time?"

"Angela…"

The Compact

"It's—I don't want to talk to a teacher outside of school…It ruins the idea they live there."

He rolls his eyes and tosses a pair of clean socks at me from off my desk. "Too bad. The spark plugs are by the back door. Take them and remember, one this afternoon is when you turn into a pumpkin again, okay?"

"Yes, sir." When the door shuts, I gulp the rest of the food and peel out of my nasty clothes, tossing them into the hamper before I slip on my plush robe. I bury my nose in the purple collar and take a deep breath enjoying the faint scent of vanilla on it. *I'll need to refresh this soon. I hate it when Mom's perfume fades.*

In the bathroom, I twist the shower nob until the mirror fogs, take off my boot and prop it against the outside of the tub,

The Compact

balancing on one foot beneath the scalding water until the previous night rinses down the drain, though, by the time I get out, my temper simmers. *I can't believe Ronni put Oliver in The Shadow's path! He might have gotten him killed...unless that was the idea.* A chill washes over me, and I snuggle into my robe and tie the belt, slipping on my boot again. While I towel off my hair, I push off the concept. "Ronni is a lot of things, but a monster isn't one of them…"

In my room, I rip a page from my journal and scribble a note to Ronni. *For that stunt. He can drop off the spark plugs to Mr. Beezly. Assuming he's around today.*

I throw on a fresh pair of jeans and a sweatshirt, raising the hood and tackle the stairs. *Gravity, plus down the stairs, plus a boot, is a weird combination. Not my favorite.*

The Compact

With the spark plugs in the front pocket of my sweatshirt with the note, I pedal straight through the center of town and pass the turn-off to head toward the neighborhood Mr. Beezly and Oliver share and into the sleeping farmlands. I pause at the edge of one empty field and count five rows to the right and fifty-five feet away from the road, finding the lumpy boulder Ronni mentioned. *Thankfully, the farmer is too cheap to have it removed, and too lazy to do it himself.* I move to the far side of it and dig into the soft earth to find the metal box Ronni buried. Pulling it out, I pop the spark plugs and note into it and rebury it. *If these are still here when I check tomorrow, I will not be happy.*

Getting on my bike once again, I pedal a bit faster. *If I'm quick about it, I can grab Oliver's bike for him and still have*

The Compact

time. The sun is high in the sky by the time I pull onto the plot of land the factory occupies. I can't even bring myself to look at the crumbling structure. Hurrying to Oliver's bike, I manage to keep a grip on one of his handlebars and run it alongside me. *It's the least I owe the kid after saving my butt.*

Once I'm on the paved road again, I coast and rub my throat. A part of me can still feel the creature's rough grasp. I drift down the slight hill which leads into *Canallia Glen,* the uppity neighborhood the mayor insisted local banks invest in on behalf of his wife's family's real estate business a couple of years ago.

I scan the rows of houses, cruising the even sidewalks until I catch sight of a pile of broken-down cardboard boxes by a trash can. *Bingo.* Propping my bike by the

The Compact

blue roofed mail-box—*Nice touch*—I leave his against the garage door and go to ring their doorbell. I press the button and the theme-song from *Star Trek* plays a few bars inside. *Is it my imagination, or do they love to customize stuff?*

When the door opens, Oliver beams. "Enter, my friend!" He moves aside and swings his arm in gesture to the hallway.

A man pops his head around the corner of the arch at the far end of the hall. "Hello."

Oliver bounces by me and waves for me to follow. "This is my friend, Angela. Angela, my father, Oliver Senior."

The man pulls off a tan oven mitt for a handshake, his eyes the same bright shade as his son's. "A pleasure to meet the, young lady, who has made such an impression on my offspring."

The Compact

When Oliver flushes, I bite my tongue to keep from laughing. *Oliver, you are too pure.* I elbow him with a smile. "He's a good egg."

"I hear voices," a woman's sing-song voice comes from behind me, and I spin to find a four-foot-tall woman with red hair to her waist beaming up at me.

"Angela, I'm pleased to introduce my mother, Pamela."

I shake her hand. *And people say I'm height challenged!*

Her eyes twinkle. "I love holding hands, but you can let go now unless you want to come with me to the fridge."

Heat floods my cheeks, and I jerk away. "Sorry."

She winks and waves me off. When she saunters by me, I see how round her belly is. "The baby wants chocolate milk."

The Compact

Senior chuckles. "Baby does, or you do?"

"Everything is for the baby." She turns her attention to me once more. "If you have any questions about little people, ask away! I'm not ashamed, and you shouldn't be shy."

"*Mother*," Oliver makes a slashing motion at his throat.

"Oh, stop it Ollie. I haven't seen a single little person in town, and I'll wager your friend hasn't met one until today. What do I always say about learning and teachable moments?"

He stuffs his hands into the pockets of his jeans. "You miss your chance to serve the world when you pass up an opportunity to learn, or to teach."

She winks. "One day, you shall surpass me, young *Padawan*."

The Compact

"Hey! No garbage talk!" Senior says.

Oliver leans toward me and lowers his voice. "*Star Trek* versus *Star Wars*, choose your side and be prepared day and night to do battle for your alliance."

I clap a palm on my mouth to smother a laugh.

Pamela pulls out the milk and drags a stepstool to the counter, climbing onto it to retrieve a glass from the cupboard. When she has her milk poured, she salutes me with the glass. "If you have questions, Ollie knows where I'll be."

When his mom leaves, Oliver tugs on my sleeve. "Follow me." He tilts his head the way we came. "We're going to study," he says a bit louder.

Senior's brows dip. "I wasn't aware you'd taken on any sophomore classes, Junior."

The Compact

"I didn't—" His eyes dart to me and the air presses in. "Angela doesn't own a computer. I offered for her to use mine for a class project."

Senior beams. "Good man. Have fun, kids. Holler if you require anything."

Oliver leads me to an offshoot in the hallway I hadn't noticed, a bright tangerine colored door at the far end. "My room is the most fantastic one in the house."

I can't help but return his grin. "Is orange your favorite color?"

He twists one of his curls around his finger. "Yes, in fact."

In his room, he shoves a pile of clothes off an extra chair against the wall and pushes it toward his desk before he takes a seat in the swiveling computer chair. He lets his momentum spin him a few times with a laugh.

The Compact

I peek at the hall and lower my voice. "You're handling this a lot better than I'd have expected."

He beams. "There are multiple factors we don't know, but we're certain it can be hurt, and light is a weakness. If it has one, it may have more and anything with a weakness can be beaten." He taps away at his keyboard as if the issue is settled for him.

"But what if it can't?"

He scowls and scratches his chin. "Impossible. Any living creature is guided by natural laws. They cannot be undone, anymore than energy can be destroyed."

I shake my head. *Is this kid a superhero?* "Even after what you saw last night, you're not scared?"

His neck reddens and he studies his pants. "To feel fear and to allow it to dictate

The Compact

your actions are two separate and distinct concepts. Do I feel fear? Of course. Will I allow it to control me? No. As long as I draw breath, I have a chance to help you beat this...Shadow creature. A shadow by its own nature cannot abide in a space the light occupies. I intend to bring the light to it." He straightens his spine and puffs out his chest.

Tears sting my eyes. *I don't know if this kid is crazy or inspired, but I like the way he thinks.*

We type and search for what seems an eternity until the alarm on my phone goes off.

"That's my cue."

Oliver scans the list of details I'd helped him compile. "You can't think of anything else?"

The Compact

"If I do, I'll let you know." I chew my lip.

"Here..." He opens the drawer to his desk and pulls out a dark blue metal flashlight, dropping it into my palm. "To keep you safe. Remember, we will beat this thing."

***

12:00 p.m. September 8, Springfield, Connecticut

Hurting Angela is the opposite of the plan.~ Ronni Russo

In the empty field, I crumple Angela's note and throw it to the ground, grinding it beneath my foot. "Shame on *me*? Precious Oliver is on *our* side?" I cram the

The Compact

sparkplugs into the pocket of my sweatshirt and study the cloud dotted sky. "Doesn't she get everything I do is to help her? To protect us?" I swing my leg onto my bike and dust kicks up in the wake of my tires. *What if The Shadow had killed him?* The line from her note sticks between my ears, and my guts knot. "I didn't want him dead…I wanted to scare him away." The world whistles past me. *It's not team Angela and Ronni anymore. Now it's Angela and Ollie versus all by himself, Ronni. She thinks, what? The Shadow will stop if we sympathize with it? If we shine some light on the situation?* I laugh. "It was a fluke the flashlight worked." *Life isn't rainbows. Storms leave damage, and people die. She thinks some brainiac will solve our problems? Yeah, they've tried before.*

The Compact

More than a part of me wishes Ollie took the first hint. I growl. *I've gotta move forward on my own. Gather my supplies and be done with him.*

I stand on my pedals and push harder to get up the hill, pulling up my hood to coast down the other side until I skid into the driveway of the third house on the street, a silver-ish blue sedan in the driveway. *Mr. Beeswax.* I roll my eyes and pull the hood low on my forehead. Fists in my pockets, I drag my feet to his door and press the bell with my elbow.

"Backyard," he yells.

I sink my teeth into my cheek and follow his voice. *Keep calm. Don't get yourself into trouble.*

Mr. Beezly glances from the lawnmower he's working on for some reason. He thunks it with the wrench he

The Compact

holds. "Can't put her away yet, not when she's used up." He arches a brow, and I bite my tongue. "What can I do for you?"

I hold the baggie of sparkplugs out to him.

"What? Cat got your tongue?" The edges of his mouth draw away to reveal too many teeth when he takes the plugs and pushes himself off the ground. "Hey, I'm beat. Come in for a second and have some lemonade. I'll grab the cash to send with you."

"No problem. Neighbor helping neighbor, right?"

His eyes narrow a hair and I gulp. "Right...thank him for me."

I give him a two-finger salute and back out of the yard before hopping on my bike.

The Compact

In the distance, clouds gather. *If The Shadow wants to strike in two weeks, I'll have to be ready in one.*

The Compact

Chapter Seven

12:00 a.m. September 9, Springfield, Connecticut

What would I do without him?~ Angela Miller

I study the crisp, white ceiling of my bedroom, my mind circling at a hundred miles a minute. *What if it's not some crypto—whatever like Oliver said. What if it's something else? Something darker?* My pulse picks up it's pace, and I shift my attention out my window to the moon. *I have to know but—wait. The journal. Ronni and I used journals to communicate in secret when we were kids.* Rising, I hobble to my desk and pull open a few drawers. *If I can find the ones we used, I can get*

The Compact

something solid for Oliver to work with. I grab the flashlight he gave me off my desk and flip it on rather than risk Dad seeing my bedroom light beneath the door on a pilgrimage to the bathroom.

I tuck the light between my jaw and shoulder and pull open the bottom drawer. It's deep and wide, packed to the brim with journals I'd scribbled my thoughts in throughout my life. *Why couldn't I have been a kid who used one journal a year? Whichever one I need might be anywhere!* I dig through the colorful covers and peer at the dates on each first entry. *For the love of letters to myself, where is twenty-twelve?* The pile of books grows at my side until only one remains in the drawer. *Please be it, please be it, please—* "Twenty fourteen?" I groan. *There have to be more journals but where—* I smack my forehead. *The Dumont*

The Compact

house! That time is such a blur…I had to have left them there. I gulp and look out the window. *Dad still insists he drives me to and from school right now.* My stomach knots. *If I'm going to nab that journal…it has to be now.*

Dragging on a ripped pair of jeans, I exchange my nightgown for a sweatshirt and hesitate before opening one bottom drawer in my dresser. I pull out Mom's purple scarf and wrap it at my throat. The idea of feeling its fingers on me again would be enough to keep me home. *Don't let fear decide your actions. Oliver is right. Keep moving.* I take a deep breath and creep downstairs and out to the garage, pocketing Dad's house keys so I don't leave the house unlocked and him exposed. *I'm doing this for all of us, Dad.* In the driveway, I pause looking at his window.

The Compact

What would he do if I never came home? What would I do without him?

I don't allow myself to consider the way my pulse races, about the eyes I can feel drilling into my back from each dark recess, or my instincts telling me to turn home. I keep going and clutch my flashlight until the rough texture of it bites into my palm.

The potholed road is near impossible to navigate at night, no matter how bright the moon tries to shine. At one point, I zig instead of zag to avoid a pothole and nearly end up in the deep ditch which runs alongside the road to the cul-de-sac. I slam on the breaks and drop my feet to the ground while my vision swims. A dizzy spell slams me, and I dig the butts of my palms into my eyes until it passes. *Maybe not taking my*

The Compact

meds today wasn't the best decision...no matter how they make me feel.

Something moves behind me, and I whirl to find a few leaves being pushed across the pavement. I switch on my flashlight to shine it at them, but they keep moving. *It's the wind.* My hair stirs, and I take a slow breath. I walk alongside my bike the rest of the way and fiddle with the flashlight's settings until it's at full strength. *Remember what Oliver said, the battery will only last an hour before it has to be recharged when it's used at full strength.* I swallow the knot in my throat and keep moving.

Trees sway in the wind to scrape against abandoned houses, and I swing the beam of the light in a wide arc. The nerves beneath my skin bristle, waiting for whatever hides in the dark. *It's a big town. It*

The Compact

may not even be here...right—what if there's more than one? My heart hammers against my ribs as I reach the wrought iron gate to our old driveway. It still stands open from my last rushed visit. *Here's hoping Mom doesn't find me again.* I gulp, my feet cemented in place. The overgrown trees, still heavy with yellow leaves, arch over the driveway to blot out the moon. *You can do this...it can't stand any light. Don't let the shadows scare you away from the truth.*

I hold my breath, my ears strained for the slightest movement while cold sweat trickles down the back of my neck. *Where's Ronni when you need him?* I hurry along the path and keep my steps light until I reach the porch. Propping my bike against the wooden banister, its paint like flaking skin, I scurry up the groaning steps. My booted foot crashes through a bad spot in the wood and

The Compact

my scream echoes through the night. I clamp a palm over my mouth. When nothing happens, I grab the still solid wooden post which holds the porch roof and wrench my leg free. I sink my teeth into my lip and head inside. Shutting the door behind me, I force the rusty deadbolt into place. *A lot of help it'll be if ten feet of hungry monster wants inside.* I brush off the idea and tiptoe to the staircase in the living room.

My flashlight casts lengthy shadows from the furniture left to rot, antique hutches with shattered windows and couches coated in dust. Springs poke through the once comfy cushions where mice have made their homes. The scent of ammonia overwhelms me, and I cover my nose. My family's memories litter each inch of the space, though I walk through most of them as a stranger. *What happened here? Why did we*

The Compact

leave? No matter how far into my memory I reach, I hit dead ends and brick walls. *Why can't I remember?*

I mount the spiral staircase and test each step before I trust it. *The last thing I need is to bring the whole house down on top of me.*

A large circular, moth eaten, rug covers the wooden floor at the top of the stairs. The landing leads to halls on either side. *Mom and Dad's room was...* I swing my light down the right hall. *This way... Which makes the door on the right side of that hall Mom's office.*

The house creaks, and I arch my light across the floor below but find nothing. Swallowing, I venture down the left hall and study the three doors. The walls are covered in drawings. My light catches on one of two girls with a mom and a dad outside our

The Compact

house, the sun beaming on our squiggled faces. *Mom was furious when I drew this—this is my room.* The door isn't latched, and I press my palm to the cool wood; it swings inward with a bit of force.

The curtains lay in a heap beneath the open window; a pale light floods the room. I lower the level of my flashlight. *It's bright enough in here that I can conserve some battery.* Sun-worn toys scatter the floor, the covers on the bed thrown off as if someone just left it. I lick my chapped lips and touch the mattress, letting out the breath I hold when I find it cold on my fingertips. *Okay, find it and get out.*

I pin the light between my jaw and shoulder and lift the mattress a few inches. The coating of black mold churns my stomach. Shoving away the disgust, I slide my fingers into the space and probe until I

The Compact

hit something hard. *What's—* Screaming, I fling the bone of some animal away. My light falls to the ground to roll beneath the bed. It plays on the far wall until it settles on a blood red trunk, a single hook holds the lid shut while it bounces. *What the...* I take a cautious step toward it. The closer I draw, the more it rattles. It feels like someone else's hand that reaches for the latch. The moment it's loose, I fall back, screaming when a hissing mass leaps at me. I hold my chest as an opossum bares its fangs and skitters toward the window, jumping out onto the roof.

I take a few deep breaths until I can hear my thoughts again above my pulse and fish the light out from beneath the bed, wiping the dirt off my cheek when I rise again. From inside the trunk, forgotten secrets stare at me, and I brush my fingertips

The Compact

across the lips of a cracked China doll. *My grandma bought me this when I was what, two?* I set it aside and keep digging. I find teddy bears who leak stuffing and mouse droppings, fairy tales with missing pages, and a few blankets. At the bottom of the box, I find a single book bound in black. I open it to the first page. *Found you! February tenth, twenty-twelve.*

***

7:30 a.m. September 9, Springfield, Connecticut

What a tool.~ Ronni Russo

Other students shuffle by me, and I yawn with a blink, a book beneath my arm while the bell rings. I check my watch.

The Compact

Lucky me, I'm in time for my brain to be melted. Awesome. I straighten my back and pull from the locker what I need for math.

"Hi! I hoped I'd catch you."

Who is stupid enough to talk to me? I pull myself to my full height and turn to find Oliver.

Be nice. For Angela's sake... "Hello Olli—Oliver. You said you hate to be called Ollie, right?"

He bobs his head and straightens his suspenders. "I'm glad I caught you ahead of class."

"Any specific reason in mind?" I resist the urge to lean against the lockers and fold my arms.

"Yeah, about the—" He looks one way and then the other, lowering his voice as if we're friends. "The Shadow."

"Have questions on how not to die?"

The Compact

He raises a brow. "No—I—I wish to query you on the possible locations of any nuclear waste treatment plants, or perhaps government research facilities? I thought, perhaps, if there was one nearby, the origin of The Shadow might be more scientific than first considered to be."

I tilt my head. "You're really in on this, aren't you?"

He beams. "Most assuredly! If there is any way in which I can be of assistance, I'm appreciative as the *new kid*. I do love a puzzle."

"You're not upset about the other night?"

"I had been." He puffs out his cheeks and studies his shoes for a second. "What's done is done, though. I cannot live in what has happened."

The Compact

I bite my tongue to keep from laughing in his face. "Sure. I gotta get to class."

"What about my query?" He jogs a couple of steps to fall into line beside me while I head for the unused hallways.

"About?"

"The facilities about town that may lead to events of a nature in which the scientific and supernatural merge."

I jam my thumbs into my closed eyes until I see spots. *Is this kid for real?* "No. There aren't. The Shadow—he's not—you can't put his existence off on things you *understand*."

"He? His? It's a male? Are you certain?"

I roll my eyes. "Yes, I am."

"How? Have you seen a female of the species? Are there distinguishing

The Compact

characteristics? You've said it's humanoid but—"

I grab his arm, quickly easing my grasp. "I gotta get to class. Bye, kid! Oliver!" I wave over my shoulder. *What a tool.*

***

2:00 p.m. September 9, Springfield, Connecticut

Bless your pure, pure soul.~ Angela Miller

I blink at the tan roof of the truck cab. Exhaustion tugs at me. *What even happened today? Why am I exhausted—oh, yeah.* I yawn. *A tour of a girl's abandoned house will do that to her.* I shut my eyes and lean my head against the window until a

The Compact

sharp tap sends me scrambling to the other side of the cab.

"Apologies!" Oliver waves.

I scrub the haze from my vision and scoot over to pop the door open. "Hi."

"Did you feel the earthquake earlier?"

"There was an earthquake?"

He bobs his head. "It's fascinating. When my family lived in Ohio, we didn't experience anything like it. Exhilarating."

I shiver. "I'm glad I didn't notice it." *Like my life isn't freaky enough without worrying about the ground moving on its own.*

He laughs and wags his head. "This reason isn't why I sought you out, though. I desired to check on you. You didn't seem yourself today."

The Compact

I fidget with the hem of my shirt and clear my throat. "I'm tired and speaking of." Leaning, I dig through my backpack. "This is why."

He takes the journal when I offer it with pursed lips. "You want me to read your diary?" His cheeks redden.

I snicker and resist the urge to ruffle his hair. "It's from years ago, you won't run into anything mushy to embarrass you."

"Years—you mean when The Shadow first arrived?"

I bob my head. "That's what I hope. There may be information in there I've forgotten about."

"Do you have a lot of memory issues?"

I shift and run my fingers through my hair, butterflies streaking through my stomach.

The Compact

"Did I...forget something?" *Not again.*

He wags his head. "No, you've mentioned it multiple times, and thus I assumed."

I wipe my mouth with the back of my palm and study the faded elementary school, the once bright sign which welcomes students faded by the sun. "Yeah, the mind can be a weird place, I guess."

"Certainly! My mother is a psychologist. I comprehend better than most what sort of trickery it can play. You wouldn't believe some of the stories I've overheard..."

My eyes widen. "Isn't it illegal for her to share her work stuff with your dad?"

He coughs and clears his throat. "Ah, yes...but she didn't..." He laces his fingers behind his neck and scans the area around

The Compact

us. "You see, one of the hobbies I occupied my time with as a child—which my parents were less enthused with—was learning to hack their cell phones. I overheard many a conversation not meant for my ears." His cheeks flush, and he drops his gaze to his shoes. "Not my finest moment."

"You scoundrel! You rogue!"

Giggling, he beams. "I was, wasn't I?"

"Undoubtably, but your past doesn't determine your future, right?"

"Quite, right."

"Hello, there," Dad calls with a grin and a wave.

Oliver's smile turns bashful. "Good day, sir."

"Nice to meet you, young man. Angie, is this the Oliver I've been hearing

The Compact

about? Glad to see my daughter making *real* friends."

I dig my nails into the seat. *Don't take the bait.* "Oliver is one of a kind, and I'm glad he moved to town."

When Dad looks away to wave goodbye to Mr. Beezly, Oliver slips the journal into his bag and offers me a stage wink.

Bless your pure, pure soul.

"Good day, all. I must hurry home. My mother will be worried enough. See you tomorrow, Angela!" he calls behind him.

When Dad climbs into the truck, he has a bigger smile than I've seen on him in years.

"Who put extra sugar in your coffee?"

He rolls his eyes while the engine turns over. "No one. Can't a dad be happy to

The Compact

see his daughter make a decent friend? What do you say to waffles for dinner? Bring back the tradition?"

I frown and scratch at my pants. "When was that *ever* something we did?"

"When you were a child. The—" he clears his throat and forces his face toward the road. "The whole family loved it."

I chew my lip. "There's so much about when I was a kid I can't remember. Have I ever told you that?"

Without taking his attention off the road, he reaches to squeeze my wrist. "Sometimes it's best to forget the past, kiddo."

"But what if it's important to the present?"

"What do you mean?"

I take a deep breath and hug my waist. "What if The Shadow first appeared

The Compact

when Ronni and I were kids?" Dad's knuckles whiten on the wheel, but I press on when he stays quiet. "What if there's something I've forgotten that might help stop it?"

"It's *not* real, Angela. Ronni may say something, but it doesn't make it gospel. He hasn't always been—"

"But I've experienced it myself!"

He slams on the brakes to gawk at me. "What?"

I chew my bottom lip and pick at a frayed thread in the woven seat cover. "I've felt it. It had its hands at my throat. I've heard its voice."

His face pales while the muscle at his jaw twitches. "When?" A car honks behind us, but he doesn't react to it. "I asked you a question, Angela. Answer me. *Now.*"

"Dad, you—"

The Compact

"*Now.*"

"The night I got stuck out at the quarry, and again a few nights ago when Oliver—"

"Oliver?" The car passes us and speeds down the street. "Good—" He rubs his forehead. "You brought that sweet kid into—this—delusion of yours?"

"It's not!" Tears sting my eyes, and I pound my fist on the seat. "I've *heard* The Shadow, and it tried to choke me! Oliver scared it off! He sensed it there too!"

"Did he *see* it?"

"Only Ronni can see it." I wipe my nose on my sleeve. "You know that."

He presses the gas, and we ride the rest of the way home in silence. When we pull into the driveway he gets out and points at me. "You don't tell anyone else about this, do you hear me? I have to make a call.

The Compact

You get in your room, do your homework, and don't even think about leaving until I come for you. Do you hear me?"

"Dad I—"

"*Answer me.*"

I nod and he heads into the house without another word.

The Compact

Chapter Eight

12:00 p.m. September 10, Springfield, Connecticut

There's no time to waste.~ Ronni Russo

In the darkness of the bedroom, I zip my jacket and go to the window, but when I push on the frame, it doesn't budge. I grab a flashlight and shine it on the frame with a groan. *Are you kidding me, dude?* Nails stick out an inch or so on both sides to keep the window shut. *He must have done it while I was out.* I mutter beneath my breath and pull a pair of pliers out from beneath my mattress. *You're smart, but I'm smarter. If you were my real dad, you'd know that.*

The nails don't give up their place without a fight, the wood groaning like a

The Compact

stuck pig while I pry them free. When the first one pops loose, I stumble backward into the chair at the desk and freeze, listening for anything and chuckling when I don't hear a sound. *Enjoy your sleep, old man.* The second one is the same story, but this time I'm ready for it.

I tuck the nails and pliers beneath the mattress and shut the window behind me once I'm outside, the flashlight tucked into my pocket to make my descent. *This is the one time I'll give Ollie boy credit.* The moon hides behind a thick layer of clouds. I flip on the light and pedal for all I'm worth. *Even if this is enough to scare it off, I'd rather not tangle with it.*

The empty streets pass in a blur, the streetlights out halfway through the center of town. My light catches on an electrical pole broken in two. The larger top portion lies

The Compact

across the street though the lines have been removed. I slow to a stop and leave my bike a couple of yards away. Large splinters litter the ground in a halo a few feet from the base. *Those would go clean through the thickest sneaker sole.* I pick my way through them and swing the light once or twice to make sure I'm not followed. *I can't wait to be rid of him. I'll be able to live my life finally. Angela will be safe, and we can be happy.* The base of the post is stained a brownish red, the closer I draw, the stronger the smell of rot and metal grows, deep gouges travel from the halfway point of the base and continue on the broken off upper portion. I shudder and move away. *And still this town is too stupid to believe. If The Shadow has already hurt someone, there's no time to waste. I've gotta level the heart of his power.*

The Compact

The wind whips past me while I take a shortcut through the woods to the quarry, my gut flying when I take a hill too fast and catch some air. I leave my bike a ways away from the entrance rather than risk it being found by some random guard the owners hire to check in on the place every couple of months. *Any other night? Sure. But not tonight. Not when I'm this close. When it's so important.*

My thumb hovers on the switch on the flashlight. *Do I risk bringing in a security guard with the light, or The Shadow without it?* I shut it off and head for the hole in the fence. The night seems thicker with each move I make. Tree roots snag my pant legs and rocks trip me. *This is ridiculous. I'll kill myself out here before I can get the sticks.* I flick the switch one notch, a pale

The Compact

golden light giving me enough visibility to find where I'm headed.

At the top of the rubble pile, I pause to gather my bearings. *How long has it been since I went to the storage units?* I squint and catch a glint of metal in the distance when the clouds part for a split second. *Of course, it's not close.*

I keep the flashlight on and get a move on, picking my way over fissures left from years of improper mining. *Should be right—No!* My shoe kicks a pebble and sends it skittering over the edge, and I nearly follow. The earth had collapse in a massive sinkhole that merges with the quarry. "No… No. No. No. No. No. This can't be here. When did—" I smack my forehead "The earthquake." Abandoned earth movers and other equipment poke out of the dirt like souls trying to claw their way from the

The Compact

grave. A few yards off, I search the ground for a way over or some patch of dirt which doesn't look soft enough to swallow me. *Everything looks the same.* I flick the light higher until I can find the pattern of the shifted earth. The minutes tick by, and I pace looking for any way to the storage area. Growling, I rake my fingers through my hair. "This is useless. I—" The world turns upside down when the earth gives way, my flashlight flying.

I land hard on one of the submerged pieces of equipment, the wind knocked from me while my heart pounds. *How far am I from the edge of the pit?* I search the darkness for any sign of my flashlight but find none. When I attempt to climb out, the soft ground shifts beneath me to pull me in. I take a deep breath to calm my mind, but it does nothing. *I'm dead!* "Stop it. If you lose

The Compact

your head right now, you're dead." The shadows of the world above deepen, and I sniff the air. *He's coming. He must have been prowling somewhere nearby and heard me fall. I have to get out of here.* I claw at the dirt with caution until I run into the door handle for another piece of equipment. I keep digging until I find the smashed-out window of the cab. I step onto the door and test my weight; when it doesn't move, I pull my other foot onto it. My ankle twinges, but I keep going. *Ten feet to go.*

The air thickens around me. The smell of rot grows. *You gotta get out of here!* I find the top of the machine and dig. Dirt clumps beneath my fingernails, and bits of metal slice me. Once I've uncovered enough of it, I pull myself onto the roof and test the rim of the sinkhole. It crumbles beneath my palms, and the machine beneath

The Compact

me shakes. The tinkle of falling dirt meets my ears. My eyes go wide, and I claw at the edge, jumping to fling myself forward. I flatten onto the ground and crawl onto firmer earth as everything beneath me empties into the pit. A distant crash echoes as I roll onto my back and shuffle backward. A*t least I'm on the right side now.* My eyes flutter closed for a moment, and I take a deep breath. My heart aches from pumping so hard.

A hiss near my ear, hot breath on my neck, bring me to my senses. Gagging, I roll to the side before I even see him.

His pale skin glistens in the moonlight, fresh wounds blazed across his bluish skin. "So fast." He grins and drool drips from his fangs in the moonlight.

I stagger to my feet, grabbing the biggest stone I can find.

The Compact

"Hit me?" He tilts his head with fluid ease. His white eyes travel from me to the stone and back. "Fight me?" He clicks his tongue, and I hold my ground. "Go wombats…go."

"I will end you."

His tongue comes out to flick at the trail of red on his cheek. "Good luck." He steps toward me, and I fling the rock at the right side of his head with the last ounce of my arm's strength. He dodges the wrong way and his momentum pulls him into the pit while I sprint away.

I push my legs for all they're worth, the air shifting when he warps out of the hole and onto my heels. Ice shoots up my spine, my skin on fire from adrenalin.

"Tricky…child," he says, his voice near affectionate.

The Compact

Acid laps at the back of my tongue, and I run faster. The clouds part and the hulking outline of the storage shed comes into view. *Just a little farther—* Hairy fingers curl around my ankle, the wiry hair bites into my skin, and my teeth crash together as my chin hits the ground.

"Oops," The Shadow hisses.

I roll onto my back and slam my foot into his nose-less, nasty, face with a satisfying crunch. When he recoils, I scramble to my feet and keep going. I make it to the storage building and lower my shoulder to barrel through the door. The decayed deadbolt gives way, and it flies open on screaming hinges, a shower of splinters going before me.

Where are they? The Shadow howls outside, and I dive for the workbench in front of me, hurling open the first safety kit I

The Compact

find. *Please don't be too empty!* I grab a thick red flare and pop off the plastic top, striking it to the black tip of the flare. It lights without hesitation and illuminates the room. I tug down the wire feet and set it in the dirt beyond the doorway as The Shadow warps to land a foot away.

He retreats with a hiss.

Not the best idea in what used to be a room full of dynamite, but desperate times. Time to get in and get out while that thing is distracted. I sprint to the far side of the wooden floor and through a heavy door into what used to be a metal vault. Sealed crates still line the room, and I head into the farthest corner away from the water stains on the walls. *I cannot say how happy I am they expected to open this place again in a matter of months after it closed.* I grab a crowbar leaned against the wall and pop the

The Compact

lid off one of the crates. The sticks are packed in neat rows, and I grab as many as I can carry, looping a few ropes of fuse over my arm. I peek into the other room and find The Shadow with his fists curled at his sides, glaring at the flare.

"No way...out," he says.

That's what you think. I keep to the wall, hidden from the view of the windows and make for the rear exit. The air outside seems twenty degrees cooler and some part of my brain wonders if I'm not in shock. *No time to wonder about it now.* I make it to my bike and keep the chords on my arm, shoving the sticks into my pockets, and trying to hold what doesn't fit. *Wombats?* The word echoes in my mind and a blanket of ice wraps me. *I know where his power is coming from!*

The Compact

***

9:00 a.m. September 10, Springfield, Connecticut

I have to find out what The Shadow's plan is.~ Angela Miller

I yawn at the kitchen table and lay my head on my arms. "School is shut down again why?" *Not that I'm upset about it, but I'd love to know what Oliver's found.* When I yawn again Dad clicks his tongue at me.

"Did you sleep alright last night, kiddo?"

I scratch the back of my head. "To my memory." *I mean, I don't remember being awake.*

The Compact

He comes to the table and presses the butt of his palm to my forehead. "You're not warm. How's the ankle?"

I reach and tap on the boot. "Strong enough, I guess."

"How's your head? Any nausea, vomiting, problems out the poop shooter?"

I cringe and bat him away. "And you're a scientist? No." *Gross.*

"You know we have to watch out for side-effects. Maybe you ought to spend the day in bed."

No way! I have to find out what The Shadow's plan is. I push away from the table and when I rise, everything wobbles. I fall into Dad's arms, his eyes wide.

"Okay, you've settled it. To bed. Now."

***

The Compact

6:00 p.m. September 10, Springfield, Connecticut

That's me…but I don't know them.~ Angela Miller

"Angie? Sweetheart? Are you awake?"

The mattress sinks beside me, and I crack an eye open. I swear my eyelids and limbs are eighty pounds heavier.

"You've been asleep all day, and your friend Oliver is here."

Some of the fog lifts from my mind, and I push myself up. The room spins again.

"Woah." I shut my eyes.

"You're not getting out of bed."

"But I—"

"He can visit you here."

The Compact

He leaves and a few minutes later there's a soft knock on my door. When it swings open, Oliver slips into my room and leaves the door open a crack.

"Hey, stranger."

His eyes widen when they land on me. "You appear, unwell."

I smirk and lean into my pillows. "I feel worse, I promise."

He scratches at his head, and I spy the journal tucked beneath his arm. "Find anything interesting?"

He pops onto his heels with his hand in his pocket. "Not yet. Mother and Father have had me busy with chores for most of the day. However, I found one item I wished to bring to you." He comes and perches on the edge of my mattress to pull the journal from beneath his arm, the ruby red ribbon place holder tucked a few pages in. He taps

The Compact

the book with his index finger. "You, Ronni, and a child named Richard, Richie for short, were quite close, weren't you? I take it the boys are twins?"

"I—" I massage the pressure building in my temples. "Ronni doesn't have a brother...he—I...ouch!" Fire burns behind my eyes, and I wince.

"Angela, are you alright?" He rubs my arm.

"I need something for my head."

He scurries out of the room and returns a few moments later with a glass of water and a couple of *Advil*.

I wash them down, a cold sweat breaking over me. "Ronni doesn't have a brother—he—I don't—" My thoughts tangle.

His brows sink, and he pulls something from the book. He places an old

The Compact

photo on my lap. A young girl and two identical boys beam at me.

"That's me." I point to the pigtailed girl before my finger trails to the boys. "But I don't know them."

"But your names are on the back." He gently flips it over.

Angela/Ronni/Donni.

His frown deepens while my breath comes in short gasps before the world goes black.

The Compact

Chapter Nine

9:23 p.m. September 10, Springfield, Connecticut

I have to lead it away!~ Angela Miller

When I wake again, I'm chased from sleep by The Shadow...or at least a nightmare about it. I'm drenched in sweat, each muscle in me knots, and sleep hasn't done anything to lessen the pounding in my skull. My stomach growls. I drag myself out of bed and wait a moment to see if the room stays in place for me or not. When it doesn't move, the scent of Italian calls me downstairs.

I find Dad in the kitchen with his back to me.

The Compact

"What are you making?" I mumble and rub a crusty from my eye.

He jumps, the slotted spoon in his grasp slinging some of the tomato sauce onto the ceiling. "You're awake!" He shoos me to a seat at the table before wetting a kitchen sponge at the sink. He goes onto his tiptoes to scrub at the white plaster, managing to spread the sauce instead of clean it. "Hope you like the color pink," he mutters.

The mention of color brings Oliver to mind, and I search the kitchen. "Where did Oliver go?"

Dad spares me a glance. "I sent him home because you weren't well."

I rub at my forehead. "Did he tell you why he came?"

He lets out a slow breath, his face the color of the sauce, and wags his head.

The Compact

"Nope. Do you not remember why he came by?"

I rub my throat. *No, but if I admit to it, you'll know I haven't been taking my meds.* "He wanted to...show me something." A hazy memory surfaces. *Wait...* A plate of pasta appears in front of me to pull me from my thoughts. "Have I been out long?"

"Most of the day," he says and settles in with his own plate. The feet of his chair screech across the linoleum.

A flash of a photograph surfaces in my mind and my stomach churns. "Did—did Ronni drop in? He didn't leave me a note?"

He scowls while he picks at his food. "Not that I'm aware of, and for all I care, I hope I never see him again. He's aggressive, and flippant; no respect whatsoever."

The Compact

"He's a part of me, Dad." I fold my arms.

He shuts his eyes while the vein in his temple throbs before he lets out a slow breath. "Do not—he isn't. He *ought* to be dealt with."

I swallow and pick at my food. "Can I—may I ask you a question?"

He quirks a brow. "You did."

I smack my forehead and groan. "You're going to give me mood whiplash."

Dropping his fork, he pinches the bridge of his nose. "I'm sorry, kiddo. I love you, Angie, and I hope I don't ever make you forget it. You mean more to me than the stars in the sky, the grains of sand in the ocean, and the hairs on your head combined. I don't mean to be an ogre about this. I want what's best for you. Do you understand?"

The Compact

I bob my head. "I love you too, Dad."

"Now, what's your question?"

I bite my lip and push the food around my plate, my heart beating a bit harder. "It's about Ronni..." I clear my throat. "Did he ever mention he has a brother? To you, I mean."

He shoves a massive bite into his mouth and slowly chews.

He's stalling. Why?

When he swallows, he studies the tablecloth and picks at a stain. "No, he hasn't mentioned one to me."

"Dad?" I lean and tilt my head until my hair is nearly on my plate. Still he won't meet my eyes. "What aren't you telling me?"

The Compact

"Bah!" He waves me off. "It's in your head, kiddo. Eat your dinner. You've...been through enough today."

"It's *not* in my head!" I slam my fist on the table, making our plates rattle.

He opens his eyes wide and stares at me. "There. Does this satisfy you? Am I truthful enough for you now? Ronni did not drop by and has not mentioned a brother."

"What about Sophie, or Mom? Have they—"

"No! Don't bring them into this. Candice and Sophie haven't said anything. I'm not your go-between—"

"But you..." The words die on my tongue when something on the breeze tickles my nose. "Do you smell that?" The hair on my arms raises, and I run to the window above the sink, peering into the night. Rot mixed with copper and ammonia steeps my

The Compact

senses. The lights flicker while tears gather in my eyes. *Not here. Dad doesn't even believe me. I have to lead it away!* When I head for the back door, he grabs my wrist.

"Where are you headed?"

"Let go of me!" I try to tug away from him. "It's here!"

He stands to take hold of my shoulders and searches my face. "What is?"

"The Shadow! I can smell it. It's coming. I have to lead it away!" I push away from him with all my strength, but his grip on me tightens. My breath comes in short gasps. "It's—going to—kill you. I have to—lead it away."

Tears gather on his lashes, and he pulls me tight to his chest.

I fight harder. "I can't let it hurt you! You're all—"

The Compact

He hushes me and strokes my hair. "Easy now."

My heart hammers even harder, and I thrash in his arms while the dishes on the table rattle. "I have to go! It'll kill you. It's going to kill you!" The scent of death overpowers my senses, even as I feel the world slip away.

***

??? September 10, Springfield, Connecticut

I'm sorry I let it hurt you.~ Angela Miller

Something warm and wet drips on my cheek when I float to consciousness once more.

"Come back to me, Angie. Come back."

The Compact

The world rocks as I open my eyes, reaching to my cheek. When I study my fingers, they're coated in blood. "Dad?" My voice is hoarse, my throat sore.

"Angela!" The relief packed into one-word tears at my heart. "Thank God, you're alive."

When my vision focuses, I freeze. Thick welts trail his throat, egg sized bruises forming dark and angry on his jaw and cheeks while blood drips from his nose. His shirt is torn from top to bottom and more blood streaks the fabric. I touch one swollen eye and my tears flow. I cling to him. "Do you believe me now? It's not safe! It's real. The Shadow is real, and it will destroy everything!"

He gathers me off the ground and rises to his feet. A strangled sob echoes in my ears.

The Compact

"I'm sorry... I should have listened to you." He kisses the top of my head and carries me upstairs.

Over his shoulder, I spy the broken window above the sink. "Did it get in?"

"No, baby." His voice is soft against the top of my head.

"Can you see it too?"

He hesitates at the top of the stairs. "Yes."

My lip trembles, and I bury my face in his neck. "I'm sorry, Dad. I should have listened to Ronni. I—"

He hushes me when my tears make me hiccup and carries me to my room. "Stay here, my brave, brave girl." He sits me on the bed and kisses my forehead.

My blood runs cold when he backs away, and I catch sight of the deep gash in his arm. Dried blood matts the hair there.

The Compact

"I'll find the first aid kit and clean us both up, and then I'll board up the window until I can fix it tomorrow."

I probe my split lip and wince. "I'm sorry I let it hurt you."

Freezing in the doorway, he shifts to study me again, his voice soft, "No, baby. You helped me fight it off. If not for you, it would have killed us both."

***

2:40 a.m. September 11, Springfield, Connecticut

Deliverance is destruction.~ Ronni Russo

I pry loose the nails again, my backpack heavy with dynamite and everything else I'll need. *He attacked*

The Compact

Angela. In her own home, he put his grubby fingers on her. Again! I'm putting an end to this—to him—once and for all.

I wince when I land, my body sore from the fight. I touch the bruise on my cheek. *In a few days, you'll finally be on the other side of this.*

I don't dare to let my attention linger on any one shadow; my stomach is in knots, and heart is in my throat when I bike down the street. The town still hasn't fixed the powerlines, so the lights on one side of the street remain dark. I keep to the lighted side and pedal harder from one halo to the next. *He'll be onto me soon if he isn't already.*

When I round the corner, the moon outlines two low, elongated buildings. *Get in, place the charges, get to safety, and wait. You'll know when the time is right.*

The Compact

I pedal to the rear of the building and prop my bike against the brick wall. Pushing aside a gate, I climb onto the dumpster, and from there I pull myself onto a nearby tree branch. It bows beneath my weight, but it's thick enough it doesn't snap. The clouds pass in front of the moon, and my pulse spikes. *Deep breaths. This will be done with soon.* I swing my backpack onto the roof and follow it a moment later. Gravel crunches beneath me. Pausing, I sniff the sweet air of the night and strain my ears. "Goal one, complete," I say. I stagger to my feet and wipe the sweat from my brow. Walking to the sky light, I smirk when I find the penny I'd left still in its place. I pinch it and lift it to the sky light with a laugh. *This town is full of blind idiots.*

My thud like a thunderclap in the stillness, I drop onto the pressed wood table;

The Compact

a cartoon wombat emblazoned beneath my feet. I rush to hide behind a bookcase until I'm sure the security guard didn't hear me. *No shock there, he's half deaf, but a guy can't be too careful.*

    I steal my way through silent hallways by memory until I come to my first destination, the principal's office. The idiot doesn't ever remember to lock her door, and I saunter inside. Taking the hammer and crowbar from my backpack, I pry up the carpet and the wooden floorboard beneath. *Thank you, Town Council, for not allotting enough money for this place to be demolished and replaced with proper foundations.* I set the first few sticks equipped with cord and trigger before I cover them and hammer the board into place again, tacking the carpet with a penny nail.

The Compact

I slip by the security guard to place a few sticks in my locker, and the third and final batch, in Mr. Beezly's classroom. I tape a stick at a time to the underside of his desk, making sure the cords are taped out of sight. "The last thing I want is for him to find them and spoil the surprise."

There will be innocent kids here... I swallow and push the idea away. *As long as this school operates, The Shadow will always live. He'd kill more people than I will.* I double check what channel the radio is set to and splice the third set of fuses into it.

Now we wait. Deliverance is destruction.

***

The Compact

8:00 a.m. September 11, Springfield, Connecticut

They always get it wrong.~ Ronni Miller

"Angela?" A voice calls, drawing me from sleep. "Angela, are you here?"

I drag open my eyes, and my vision focuses on the spiderweb coated ceiling of the cul-de-sac house. Sunlight filters through the window to catch the dew which coats them. *They're almost beautiful.*

"Angela?"

I groan and roll out of bed, a layer of dust disturbed in the process floats into the air, and I cough and wave a palm to dispel it. The ancient floors groan beneath my weight, and I study the radio in my hand. *You'll know when the moment is right; you'll sense*

The Compact

when he's there. I keep a light hold on it. *Not yet.*

"Angela—"

I peer over the banister into the dingy living room below to find red curls sticking through a dark blue bicycle helmet.

I've had enough of this kid, no matter what Angela says. "What are you doing here?" I sneer.

He blinks at me while his brows dip low.

"How did you find this place, *Ollie boy*?"

"The journal. An—Ronni?"

I beam and take a bow. "Of course, kid. What can I do for you?" I saunter down the stairs stopping at the bottom to lean against the banister post.

He blinks and rubs his forehead. "Is Angela here? I—everyone is concerned

The Compact

about her safety. She wasn't home when her dad went to awaken her this morning."

I chuckle. "No, duh, genius." I run fingers through my hair and make a move toward him.

"Angela!" He scoots backward. His knees hit the couch, and he falls onto it, releasing a shower of dirt.

"What? Don't want to talk to me, Ollie boy?"

"Whatever you planned, you failed." His lip trembles while his voice wavers. "They found the bomb you planted beneath your teacher's desk."

I growl. "Why are you here, twerp?" My finger twitches toward the trigger on the radio.

"Angela! I know you're here, please! Come out!"

The Compact

I inch closer. "What if she doesn't want to play with you anymore? I protect her. Don't you know? It's been my job for years. No one else cares."

"Untrue!" Pulling a makeup compact from his pocket, he opens it with trembling fingers and holds the mirror toward me.

I touch my jaw and scowl. "I hate mirrors, they always get it wrong." The round reflection shows chestnut locks past my chin, soft pink lips, and deep chocolate eyes looking at me from beneath the hood of my sweatshirt.

"That's not true…Angela. Listen to me. *Hear* me."

The world around me spins. "She can't! Stop it!"

"Angela!"

My head throbs. I laugh and hold my temples.

The Compact

"Angela!" He flings himself at me and hugs my waist tight. "Angela, listen to me, please."

I blink.

***

I wanted one friend.~ Angela Miller

"What—Where am I?" I tremble. *The Dumont house?* "How did I—" The pressure at my waist draws my attention, and I find Oliver with a tight grip on me. My vision blurs, and it feels as if his thin arms hold me upright. "Oliver? Where are we?"

He jolts away to stare into my eyes for a moment before he beams and hugs me tight once more. "It's you! You're back. You're safe, Ronni's gone."

The Compact

My blood drains. "You met…Ronni?"

He holds me at arm's length, tears trickling as he bobs his head. "I'm aware of your D.I.D., and it's alright."

My belly churns with guilt, my face flushing while my tears come hard and fast. "I'm sorry I didn't tell you. I wanted one friend. One person in this stupid town who looked at me the way you did. No suspicion, no fear. No hate."

He wags his head. "Angela, you're not to blame. If there's one thing I've learned from my mother, it's this. What you're going through is anything except your fault. It means you were injured deeply. Possibly long enough ago you don't even know when or how. And for any difference it may make, his plan didn't

The Compact

work. The school is safe, they found the bomb."

"The what?" My thoughts swim and my attention falls to the radio in my grasp. Hazy memories, images as if viewed through a thick fog, float through my mind. I wag my head. "No, this isn't possible. I— Ronni protects me. He always has… he wouldn't hurt innocent—The Shadow. Deliverance is destruction." My heartrate spikes; two images come into sharp focus in my mind's eye. "We have to warn them. There are two more bombs!"

The Compact

Chapter 10

7:00 a.m. October 11, Springfield, Connecticut

Me, myself, and I. We are one. We are me.~ Angela Miller

The van bumps onto the curb when we pass a sign which reads *Springfield Psychiatric Hospital*. From the corner of my vision, I catch sight of a man. I turn in time to find Dad waving to me as I pass. My vision clouds, but I blink the tears away. *I made the right choice. This is where I need to be right now. I want this, for everyone. I'll be back with you soon, Dad, I promise.*

Dark clouds gather overhead, the multi-story red brick building spick and span in every way from the cut of the grass to the

The Compact

angle of the corners. When the judge gave me the option to come here instead of juvie, I had known it was the best option, and I plead no contest in exchange for the opportunity. *It's a strange experience to be charged with something you did but can hardly remember.* The fact I'd helped them locate the last two bombs helped the judge lean toward mercy. That doesn't keep the bottom from dropping out of my stomach. *You didn't hurt anyone. Don't let yourself forget it.*

When the van pulls to a stop out front of the building, I don't resist when the driver comes to help me out of the van, the metal cuffs at my wrists a constant reminder of what I am to the world.

The electric doors slide open and a familiar face greets me.

The Compact

"Doctor Wendel." The guard tips his charcoal colored hat to her.

Oliver's mom's eyes narrow when they land on the cuffs and shackles which chain me.

"You've delivered her to our custody. Your job is done. Uncuff her and you may be on your way."

Though the guard argues with her, Mrs. Wendel eventually wins, and I rub my wrists in sweet relief.

With a kind smile, she leads me inside, the pale walls bare. I don't know what else I expected.

We pass what she calls the rec room, a petite TV in the far corner, though it's off while a group of teen patients sits in a circle, a man in a tweed jacket at the head of it all.

"Will I have to do group sessions?" I wipe sweat slick palms on my jeans.

The Compact

She inclines her head while we move into an elevator. "I suspect you'll graduate to one in time, but let's not get ahead of ourselves. Everyone is unique."

I open my mouth to ask how Oliver is and shut it again. Somehow, in this setting, it feels…wrong.

On the top floor, she leads me down a narrow sterile hallway, cameras along the molding swivel to watch us, the air thick with bleach. At the end of the hall, we come to a metal door labeled D11.

"This will be your room while you're with us."

She swipes her key card through an electric pad and the door's lock blinks green. A beep echoes off the wall before the door retracts.

"Fancy." I bite my lip.

She winks. "We try."

The Compact

The room is bare, devoid of anything except a mattress, sink, and toilet. I gulp and force myself to move inside.

"You won't be in here forever." She touches my arm. "I can't imagine how scary this is."

I force one corner of my mouth upward. "I've seen worse. At least this time, it's my choice. I want to be here. I'll be able to have a blanket eventually, right?"

She inclines her head. "Yes. Once you're through your initial assessment, assuming you meet certain requirements."

"Translation, once you're certain I'm not a danger to myself. Will you be my doctor?"

"Yes. Are you alright with this arrangement?"

When I bob my head, she straightens her back. "I'll leave you to get comfortable."

The Compact

When she turns, she pauses. "Angela, I do have one question before I go."

"Yes?"

"What's your goal here?"

I bite my lip and hug my waist. "Complete integration, or as close as I'm able to come."

"You realize with it may come some dark memories."

A wave of nausea slams into me, but I bob my head. "Yes, ma'am. But after what Ronni did—What I did... ignorant *peace* isn't worth someone being hurt." *Me, myself, and I. We are one. We are me.*

The Compact

Epilogue

3:00 p.m. January 7, Springfield, Connecticut

Never in my years have I met a personality so self-aware.~ Dr. Pamela Wendel

Angela Miller sits in the chair in my office, the time I've worked with her kicking in when she blinks, and I catch the slightest shift in her posture; her back hunches a hair, her gaze narrowing the slightest bit. I only catch it because I'm looking. I start the audio recorder. "Hello, Ronni."

She props her chin in her palm. "What's up, doc?"

"How are you today?"

Her attention drifts to the cat calendar on my wall. "Not awesome. It's

The Compact

been a week since we've gotten to talk. Do you know what it's like to lose weeks of time?"

It's the longest stretch Angela has been in control yet. "Angela has lost time her whole life, has she not?"

She grits her teeth and shifts in her seat.

"Do you feel safe here, Ronni? Do you consider Angela to be protected in our care?"

"I haven't seen him here. So, sure." Her attention shifts one way then the other.

"Who are you looking for?"

"*Him.*" He lowers his voice. "Do you know he broke into Angela's house? While her dad was home? Aside from me, he's the one who protected her, for the most part."

The last time Ronni surfaced, she cycled through two more personalities

The Compact

before the session ended—Or I thought she did. Perhaps today will be the day we find the first piece to the base of this foundation.

"Who else protects her?"

She wags her head and bites her lip. "It won't happen, doc. Angela remembers more." She hugs herself. "I won't help you."

"What are you afraid for her to remember?"

She blinks again, her eyes widening, one hand goes to toy with a lock of her hair.

"Sophie?"

Angela grins and waves. "Hi, Miss Doctor!" The pitch of her voice rises.

I smile and wave in return. "Hello, Sophie. How are you today?"

She fidgets with the hem of her shirt. "I miss my daddy. Can he visit soon?"

"We might be able to arrange it." *What roll does she play?*

The Compact

"Can I color?"

"Of course." I press the intercom and call for an orderly to bring a paper and some crayons.

She moves to the floor to lie on her stomach, her feet kick back and forth in the air like a small child while she draws. I simply observe. *Perhaps these drawings will give me fresh—*

She thrusts a finished piece at me and starts on another. "Can you make sure my daddy gets it?"

"I can. Sophie do—"

"I don't want him to be sad again. Bad things happen when he's lonesome. I'll draw another for Angela too. She doesn't like to be lonely either."

I tilt my head. "Do you keep her company?"

The Compact

She beams. "I bring the happy. When the world is dark, I sprinkle fairy dust and make it sparkle!" she squeals and throws extra sheets of paper into the air.

So that's her position. Joy.

When her second work of art is done, she hands it to me. When I set it aside, she wags a finger at me while she holds her other pinky toward me. "Pinky promise!"

I hook my pinky with hers. "I promise. It'll make it to her. Now, why don't you sit in the chair like a big girl, can you do that for me? I have a few questions to ask you."

She takes a seat, her back comically straight. Like any six-year-old trying to be one of the adults.

Before I can even open my mouth, she gives a slow blink, and her micro expressions shift once more.

The Compact

Her smile dims a notch, her glittering eyes turn serene while she moves to slip one ankle behind the other.

"Mrs. Miller?"

"Doctor, call me Candice, please."

I move to mimic her posture. "Candice, of course. Forgive me for forgetting."

Her nose tips into the air a fraction.

So many minute changes. How many years did she shift from one facet of her mind to the next without anyone noticing?

"What's on your mind, doctor?"

I'm pulled from my thoughts and my cheeks warm. "I was considering your daughter."

"How is Angela?"

My heart twinges, the concern of a mother somehow natural in her voice. "She's better with each day."

The Compact

Her gaze flicks to the calendar. "It's been about two weeks since we've spoken."

I tip my chin. "It has."

"I guess it means she's learning to speak for herself… I'm happy for her. I want her to be confident, and to know her father loves her, even if he hasn't always been the best at showing it."

"What do you mean?"

"I…" Her voice trails off, her attention fixed on the wall. Her breath becomes slow, almost labored while tears trickle from her eyes.

"Candice?"

She doesn't respond.

"Angela?"

Her attention shifts to me, and I catch the same dead expression in her eyes I'd briefly seen the last time three personas

The Compact

had come to the surface. "No," she says, the one word a whispered hiss.

"My name is Doctor Pamela Wendel. You're safe here."

"Am....I?" She tilts her head.

"I assure you, you—and Angela—both are. May I ask your name?"

"I have…no name…though one…was given." Her attention lolls from one place to the next, her tears never ceasing, though they don't seem to bother her.

"Who gave you a name?"

"Ronni."

"What did he call you?"

"Shadow."

I dig my nails into the arm of the chair. Oliver's stories returning of his own encounters with this. *But the way he described it… I had been certain it was a*

The Compact

hallucination. Though, for Ronni, he may have been. I wonder... "Are you aware of your role?"

"Role?" Her gaze slowly shifts to me. "Explain."

"Do you know about the others?"

"They write...notes...four...I enjoy...them."

I bob my head. "Yes, and you are the fifth."

"You mentioned...roles...explain." Her fingernails tap on the arms of her chair with a rhythmic fluidity.

"Ronni protects her, Candice advocates and cares for her, while Sophie is her friend and keeps her world from becoming too dark."

She hums, a noise deep in her throat. "Protect."

Fascinating... "In what way?"

The Compact

"I am…details…"

I take a slow breath and force down my excitement. *Never in my years have I met a personality so self-aware.* "Can you elaborate?"

"The…pain…the…deaths…"

"Whose?"

She pauses, her eyes heavy on me. "Ronni's…Mother's…Sophie's…"

I bite my tongue. *This is more than she's ever revealed. Don't push. She may not be able to handle much more.*

She blinks again. Her attention darts through the room while she retreats into the seat.

"Angela? Angela, look at me." When we make eye contact, she relaxes for a moment before retching. She grabs for the bucket beside her chair and vomits into it.

The Compact

I hold a finger beneath my nose, looking away and taking a slow breath through my mouth.

When she's finished, she sets the bucket aside, and I hand her a tissue. "Angela? Can you tell me what's wrong?"

Her tears flow in earnest while her breath comes in hitched gasps.

I get to my feet and go to her, helping her put her head between her knees. "Deep breaths. Find three things you can see, three things you can hear, and three things you can touch."

Her fingers fly to mine and cling to me with a death grip. After a moment, her breath slows, though it's still ragged. "The circles on the carpet, the laces on my shoes, and the ketchup stain on my shirt; the heater, the clock ticking on the wall, the static on your radio; your hand, my heartbeat at my

The Compact

throat, and the chair I'm sitting in." A few moments pass, and she straightens in her seat, though her tears still fall.

When she releases me, I take my seat once more. "Can you tell me what's happening for you right now?"

"I remember." Her fingers dig into the fabric of her shirt and pull it away from her body. I wait and when she's ready, she continues. "His fingers..." her lip trembles.

"Whose fingers?"

"The Shadow's...everything about him," her skin blanches, "is a detail. Some memory." She swipes at the snot trail from her nose and hugs her knees to her chest. "When my mom and my sister died...my dad lost it. At five, I dug through the garbage to find food. It was covered in spiders...like his fingers." She shuts her eyes and slumps into her seat.

The Compact

"Angela, drink some water. If you want, we can continue tomorrow."

She sips from the glass beside her chair. "No. It can't rattle in my head anymore. His eyes were white because the day my mother died..." She digs her nails into her jeans. "We were in the car, and something happened to her. Her eyes rolled into her head and our car ran off into a ditch."

My heart twists.

"I was stuck there with her and begged for her to wake up for hours until Dad found us. She lost control of her functions when she died, and the car smelled horrible." She trembles and grits her teeth as she continues. "His eyes didn't stop bleeding because Ronni—" She chokes on a sob. "Ronni! He was my friend! He and his twin brother lived next door. They were

The Compact

playing with a ball in the cul-de-sac. It rolled out into the street, and I wanted to get it. Ronni told me not to go into the street without a grown-up—but Donni did! He ran to get the ball. He didn't see Momma's car—" her voice breaks off in another wail. "Ronni pushed him out of the way...but Momma hit him. When he landed, his eyes were bleeding." She covers her mouth. "Sophie!" she shrieks. "We were playing in the front yard by the gate with Momma, but she left us to make a snack for us. She said I was in charge, but I let Sophie get taken! I stood there and watched! I watched while..."

Her face goes slack and for a moment I'm worried she'll pass out until she grabs the bucket and heaves into it again.

"He took her," she shrieks between spells of vomiting.

The Compact

"Who did?"

The articles I'd read about her missing sister filter through my mind. *Whoever took her hasn't been caught.*

The bucket in her lap, she collapses into the seat, trembling. "He had a blue gray car, like The Shadow's skin, and when they called Momma and Daddy in to identify her body, they couldn't find a sitter. I had to go too. Animals had—animals had—" Her words devolve into a scream.

Scavengers go for the soft parts. My stomach rolls, and I touch my lips. It takes everything in me to maintain composure. *She needs you. Stay strong.*

"And when my dad lost custody, *he* was who the foster system handed me to, and for months he took me to the cement factory and told me what he'd done to her *there,* while he did the same things to me!

The Compact

He kept her doll as some sick trophy." She throws her head back and sobs.

The rules of these situation flit through my mind as I rise from my seat and go to her. Pulling the trash can from her, I tug the child into my arms to cry on my shoulder. I don't speak, I hold her until her tears ebb.

"I need to know his name," I say, doing my best to keep my voice even.

"Alexander Beezly."

The Compact

Justina Luther has never been one to fit into any one box; as a girl she was a tomboy in high heels.

Raised in a house that didn't swear, she keeps her books the same way. While she won't write a scene that would make your grandma blush, her words will push your emotions to the brink with twists you'll never see coming.

The Compact

From thrillers to romance, fantasy, and horror, she goes where her imagination leads, writing characters with integrity, transparency, and flaws, who don't quite fit the box.

A Crazy Ink Exclusive author, she has several titles under her belt including:

The Step Into Darkness Series:
Would You Have Believed Me?
Gut Check
The Future Looks Forward
Echoes of the Past
New Wounds
Solo Titles:
The Heart recalls
Cherry Sunrises
With short stories featured in:
Beyond Atlantis, A Crazy Ink Anthology

The Compact

Beyond The Rose, A Crazy Ink Anthology

Beyond The Beanstalk, A Crazy Ink Anthology

Beyond Fantasia, A Crazy Ink Anthology

Beyond the Mirror, A Crazy Ink Anthology.

For Melissa, An Anthology

Social Links:

Twitter: https://twitter.com/JustinaLuther aka @JustinaLuther

FB: https://www.facebook.com/authorjustinaluther/

FB reader group: https://www.facebook.com/groups/30

The Compact

2597783420625/

Goodreads: https://www.goodreads.com/user/show/8600970-justina-luther

Amazon: https://www.amazon.com/-/e/B07HR3PQJH

Blog: www.justinaluther.wordpress.com

BookBub: https://www.bookbub.com/profile/4166988090

Instagram: https://www.instagram.com/authorjustinaluther/

Pinterest: https://www.pinterest.com/justinaluther/

MeWe: mewe.com/i/justinaluther

The Compact

TikTok: http://tiktok.com/@justinaluther

Website:

www.authorjustinaluther.weebly.com

Justina Luther
Clean stories with thrilling twists...

The Compact

CRAZY INK

Copyright © 2020 by Crazy Ink

All rights reserved. No part of this publication may be reproduced, distributed or transmitted in any form or by any means, without prior written permission.

Publisher's Note: This is a work of fiction. Names, characters, places, and incidents are a product of the author's imagination. Locales and public names are sometimes used for atmospheric purposes. Any resemblance to actual people, living or dead, or to businesses, companies, events, institutions, or locales is completely coincidental.

Made in the USA
Monee, IL
12 August 2020